PROLOGUE

Will Drake stopped his car in front of the bus station at Fort McMurray. Steve O'Rourke grabbed his backpack and got out.

"Thanks for the ride," Steve said.

"No problem. I bet you're glad you're gettin' outa here." After Steve shut the door, Will mumbled, "Hope ya don't come back either."

Steve's bus trip from the oil-sands mine in Alberta to Vancouver, British Columbia, was long and tiresome. He felt excited about going home today.

The bus arrived in Vancouver at five-thirty to congested traffic. It seemed to take the bus forever to reach the Horseshoe Ferry Terminal. Finally, the bus pulled into its parking spot at the top of the hill.

Steve looked out the bus window to see the seven o'clock ferry pulling out of its berth.

I'll never make it home before midnight, thought Steve. He got off the bus and walked to the ticket line for the next ferry.

"Plans never go as you hope they will," Steve said to the man standing behind him.

“I know what you mean,” the man said. “I had plans for a special dinner with my wife.”

“Me too,” Steve responded. “I'll have to grab something to eat here, though. My last meal was last night.”

“Have a good night.”

“Thanks. You, too." Steve bought his ticket and walked away.

He looked up the hill at well-lit restaurants and took the shortcut. He stepped off the pavement and walked towards the top of the path. The path passed a taco stand. The aroma brought him to a halt in front of the counter.

A pot-bellied man stood behind the counter with his apron strings straining over his mid-section. He asked in a high-pitched voice, “Taco?”

“Three tacos and a cola, please.”

“How about I add my special salsa?” The cook grinned.

“Sure, load 'em up.”

Steve looked away from the counter to see where he could eat. He did not see the cook conceal a sly grin as he topped off each taco with his special salsa.

“Say, do I know you?” The cook said as he handed Steve his order.

Steve looked at him and shook his head. “No. But this,” he pointed to his food, “looks and smells great.” Steve smiled.

“I hope this will hold you for a long time,” said the cook. He mumbled under his breath, “forever.”

A rickety bench nearby perfectly suited Steve’s need. He could see the ferry when it came to the dock. He ate his food rapidly and washed down the last bite of taco with his cola. There was plenty of time to make the calls—one phone call to each of the women he loved.

First, he called Marge, his wife, and made amends for his late arrival. He said, “You know my pickup is at Mom's house. I need to get it.”

“I hope your mom is okay with you coming straight home.”

“No stopping at Mom's, I promise. I love you and can't wait to get home. I'll drive as fast as my pickup will go.”

As soon as Marge hung up, he called Ethel, his mom. “I'm on the last ferry. I want to go straight home. I'll visit with you tomorrow.”

“Fine, I can wait. I would rather talk to you tomorrow, anyway.”

“Mom, please meet me at the bus station in Gibbons. I want to drive straight to Secret Cove tonight. I'm ready to get home.”

“You know I will.”

“Thanks.”

With both calls made, he walked back down to the ferry lineup. He saw the lights of the ferry approaching the berth where it docked. Unloading the cars took a while, then the people boarded.

He found a chair on the top deck. Sitting there, he thought, *I am ready to get home to my own warm, cozy bed. Sleeping alone in a single cot was no good.*

They docked forty-five minutes later; he gathered up his backpack and walked through the empty ferry and down the gangway.

The last bus had left.

He called his mom. “Sorry. Change of plans. I'll call you when I reach the landing in Gibsons. I'll walk. Sitting for so long made me want to stretch my legs.”

“Okay. I hope I can stay awake until then. I'll find a movie.”

“Please drive my pickup to the pier. I'll drop you off at your house when I head for home. We'll get about five minutes to visit. I'm so tired I can hardly speak. I know it'll be late, but late is better than never. Right?”

The road along the bay went into the town of Gibsons. The air was fresh and salty. Steve walked down the dark tree-lined street; the ferry ride was a memory. The only sounds were the swish of water hitting the rocks and his shoes crunching on the pavement. The stars and a half-moon peeked out between the trees.

He felt happy to be home as he walked steadily toward Gibsons. He took a deep breath and enjoyed the salty air in his lungs. No vehicles drove along the road at the late hour.

Ahead of him, Steve saw a man with a wet black Labrador. The dog ran along the beach from the man and back to the water's edge.

Steve suddenly felt strange.

His feet.

He had trouble walking.

Steve fell forward into the grass-filled ditch by the roadside. He rolled over onto his back and stared at the night sky.

When the man with the dog came to Steve's body, he called 911.

Chapter One

SIX MONTH EARLIER

Ethel O'Rourke had a splendid view of Secret Cove and the pier. From the deck of Marge and Steves' home, she could see the fishing boats coming to the dock. There was a trail leading to the highway.

Secret Cove was part of Halfmoon Bay. Open to the sea, large boulders bordered much of its coastline. It was hidden deep in the bay, a well-sheltered anchorage. Boulders protected the moorings from the onset of wind-blown waves. A seawall protected a pier that ran out far enough for the local anglers to dock and unloaded their catch. It proved to be the place for everyone to buy fresh fish and crabs.

Ethel thought *Secret Cove is the perfect place to live. I'm glad Marge and Steve found this place.* She remembered when her son married twelve years ago. The couple had saved enough from their jobs to purchase a home nestled in the forest on the hill overlooking the cove. A perfect place to raise a family and far enough away from the in-laws. They tried to be independent, also wishing for their families to come only when they invited them.

Ethel's husband, Ian O'Rourke, died in a fire when Steve was twelve. It was just the two of them until Steve got married. Ethel had liked the cherished position of his favorite confidant. She wanted to be included in their lives. With some things she tried too hard, she knew that. She also knew Steve worked a way to share his life, and love, with both women.

It thrilled Ethel to have Marge as her daughter-in-law. She was Steve's high school sweetheart. Marge went to business college after high school, and Steve started logging. He waited for her until she graduated from college.

Ethel had been friends with Marge's parents since their children were in elementary school. She knew Marge was a healthy, strong, hardworking person. Marge was the perfect match for Steve.

She's too much like me, Ethel thought. *We're both take-charge type women with forceful personalities. But Marge and I don't have the same interests and hobbies. We have nothing in common except Steve.*

After they married, Marge set up her own bookkeeping business. The job kept her at home most days. It called for her complete attention. Her focus could not be on their two children, Jennifer and Bobby.

They needed a babysitter, and Ethel wanted to do it. Being single, she could help whenever they needed. This was a way she could keep her son and grandchildren in her life.

Ethel hoped Marge would see her as a friend. She hoped

Marge would include her as part of the family. As far as Ethel could tell, this idea had never entered Marge’s mind.

Those were Ethel’s thoughts as she rocked and knitted on the porch, doing her job as the babysitter. Marge's cat, Q, slept on the cushion on the chair beside her. The cat adopted Ethel when she was at Steve's house.

Patti, Marge's next-door neighbor, walked out to her mailbox. She waved at Ethel before walking back to her house.

Ethel felt grateful that Marge had a kindly neighbor to help when Ethel was not available.

She watched her grandson Bobby play in the yard. She listened for her granddaughter Jennifer to finish her homework.

“I'm done with this science test and my math homework,” Jennifer announced as she came out onto the porch. “I want to see who caught the biggest fish today.” She put the homework papers in her backpack and stashed it by the door.

“Sounds good, sweetheart.”

Ethel knew Jennifer's next plan of action; a dash to the pier and check the crab traps.

The door slammed and disturbed Q's slumber as Jennifer bounded down the steps. She blew Ethel a kiss as she whizzed past.

“Exactly where do you plan to go?” Ethel asked.

“To the beach. Be back soon, homework’s done.” Jennifer said. She answered the question before Ethel could ask.

Ethel knew the answers. She wanted Marge to hear through the open window.

As she watched Jennifer run, she remembered a

conversation with Marge a few years before.

Marge had said, “I tried to keep up with Jennifer. Since birth, she’s been into, onto, and under everything. I couldn’t do my work when she was awake. Thank goodness for school. It gave me a few hours to work.”

She answered, “I can see that. She is very active and curious.”

“In school, her curiosity flamed her passion for exploring. She pushed her teachers to the edge with her questions.”

“I'm glad I don’t have to answer them.”

Coming back to the present, she watched Jennifer on the move. Her red hair tried to stay in place. Her piercing blue eyes oversaw her forward motion. Jennifer radiated warmth even on a cloudy day.

Ethel thought, *thank goodness I don't have to entertain Jennifer.*

From her rocker on the deck, she could see and hear Bobby in his rock fort. He busily killed imaginary bad guys.

Jennifer ran through the middle of his war zone on her way to the pier.

As she passed, Bobby open-fired on the invisible enemy. Imaginary bullets flew past Jennifer's head.

She turned and pointed her finger at Bobby but kept moving. “It's not nice to point guns at people,” Jennifer said.

Bobby jumped out of his war and asked eagerly, “Can I come too? I want to see what they caught.”

Bobby ran close behind her. He was six and a half with a gift of imagination. He followed Jennifer everywhere if she would let him.

He followed her down the trail to the pier.

Ethel heard Marge leave the office and go into the kitchen. It was time to start dinner.

The phone rang and Marge answered it softly.

Ethel listened to Marge's voice as she spoke. It was not soft anymore.

“No! Send it back. I don't care what she said. I don't need that rug!” Marge hung up.□

Ethel waited with bated breath.

Marge stepped out onto the porch and said nicely, “I don't want that rug. Thanks for thinking I might.” She returned to the kitchen without waiting for Ethel to respond.

Ethel knew she had done it again. She had over-stepped her position in Marge’s household. She felt the sting of words. *I got the message,* she thought. *I must stay out of their business.*

She refocused on the job, babysitting and kitting. Soon it would be time to bring the children home for dinner.

A couple of weeks prior, Ethel and Jennifer saw a new boat in the harbor. Jennifer was curious about the crabs and traps. The boat and captain interested Ethel.

He looked about ten years younger and was in great shape. With a jaunty, well-worn captain’s cap covering his short black hair and a navy-blue pea-coat with gold buttons, he had a deeply tanned face and a ready smile.

Jennifer said, “Hey, you're new here. Where did you come from? You talk funny.”

“Yes, I'm new here, mate. I just sailed in from Australia. Do you know where that is?"

"That's half a world away."

Said Ethel, 'I'm Ethel O'Rourke from Sechelt, just down the coast. Welcome."

"I'm Roland, but everyone calls me Cap't Rolly. Thanks to my wife Gracie. She gave me this handle. I named my Tahiti Ketch *Grace*."

Ethel looked around for Gracie.

"She's not here. She passed away. I'm alone."

For the next two hours, they talked to him. Ethel thought *he's a likely uncle. The children don't have any aunts and uncles. He might be a grandfather substitute for my grandchildren. They never knew their grandfather.*

She took a deep breath and exhaled her question. "Would you like to meet the rest of the family? Why don't you come for dinner? Come up when you finish anchoring your boat."

Jennifer agreed. "Yes, come to our house."

"I'll check with Marge, Jennifer's mom, and send Jennifer to get you if it's okay."

"Sounds fine. I'd like the visit. It's been a while since I've been around people much."

Ethel hoped Marge would approve. Her batting average was well below average. Ethel hurried to the house. She found Marge in the kitchen.

"Jennifer and I met a new angler named Cap't Rolly. He has been at sea for months. He's from Australia. Can we invite him to dinner?" She held her breath.

For once, her idea was approved.

“Steve would be happy to have a fishing buddy,” Marge said. “Bring him up. There's enough dinner to add someone to the table.”

Dinner went off without a hitch. Now they were all friends. A good friend was all that Ethel really wanted.

Jennifer ran to the pier every day. She waited until Cap’t Rolly shook hands with the last shoppers.

He would say, “Crabs out, money in” as he cleaned and stowed the traps on the boat’s deck.

Jennifer would start with her stories or questions, always ending with, “Can I go with you?”

Cap’t Rolly gave in to Jennifer’s pleading, to go with him to moor his boat. Once anchored, he untied the dory.

Ethel saw the gentle swells in the bay rock, *Grace*, towing its dory with two children in it. It made small ripples on the hull. Ethel knew the drill. Jennifer and Bobby loved to ride the dory to shore.

They beached the dory near his rental cabin.

Jennifer and Bobby would run up the trail to their home.

Ethel monitored the dock. Watching was her job. She waited, watching the two children running through the trees.

This was her cue to say goodbye to them. It was time to go home. Her cottage behind the Evergreen Lodge Rest Home was next door to St Mary's Hospital in Sechelt.

Ethel called goodbye from the kitchen door. “See you later!”

Not waiting for an answer, she paused to give Q a pet and walked to her car.

The drive from Marge’s dusty driveway, past Trout Lake, to Sechelt and the Evergreen Lodge, took twenty-five minutes. Time Ethel spent reliving her day.

Knowing she helped her son placated her loneliness.

Chapter Two

Ethel saw Steve sitting on her front porch with his head in his hands as she pulled into her parking spot. His broad shoulders were hunched over his drooping head. He stared at the walkway leading to her home.

Steve slowly uncurled his lanky body, stood, and walked to her car. He opened the door, helping her with her things. He did not make eye contact.

Ethel saw the distress in his actions. “Hi, kiddo. What's got you?” She asked with a concerned smile.

“You always have the right words to say to me,” Steve mumbled. “That's what I'm here to hear.”

“Come on. Let's go to the house and talk.”

Steve followed her as far as the porch steps and sat down again.

Ethel opened the door and laid her purse on the entry table. She got her knitting bag from where Steve put it on the porch. “I'll be right back,” she said as she went inside.

She came out with a six-pack of cola and handed him one as

she sat beside him.

"What's bothering you?"

Steve just sat looking at the walkway.

Ethel waited.

Steve downed most of his drink in one long guzzle.

"Well?" she prompted.

Steve buried his head in his hands. He mumbled almost incoherently. "I lost my job."

Ethel leaned over to hear his words. She repeated them to be sure she heard him correctly. "You lost your job?"

Steve looked at her. "That's right! No more logging on this coast. The company canned us all. Now, what will I do?"

Ethel took a deep breath. She needed to comprehend what he said and what it meant.

Without waiting for her answer, Steve turned to stare blankly over her yard and continued. "We dove to the superintendent's shack. He wouldn't look at us. I said, 'what's wrong?' He said, 'I don't know how to tell you boys. We're done. Kaput. They closed us down. We got a court order today. Here's your last paycheck.' I knew it would happen with all them tree-huggers making a fuss on the island. They stopped the logging there and now it's stopped here."

"What did you do?"

"We just stood there. None of us could believe what we heard." He looked at Ethel. "I jammed my pay envelope in my pocket, got in my pickup, and left."

"I'm glad you came here. I don't know what to say. With the way things are, I'm not surprised a liberal judge shut down the logging."

"This is the only job I know. I'm damn good at it! I've been a logger since I graduated from high school. How will I tell Marge?"

Ethel tried to think of something encouraging to say.

Steve shook his head. "I was so overwhelmed. I needed to process what had happened. But instead of heading to the pub for a beer, I turned and drove to your house instead."

"I'm glad you did."

"Telling you first will make telling Marge easier."

"I agree."

They sat in companionable silence.

His words took the wind out of Ethel. She could think of a lot of things people say, such as life throws you a curve ball occasionally. Or, there are a lot of things to do besides logging. But none of these platitudes seemed to carry any weight or truth. This was Steve's first bout with an unexpected problem. His life had been smooth sailing until now. Except for when his dad died.

"When your dad, as a firefighter, got the job as the supervisor on the coast, it was good pay. For one person. Too tight of a budget for a family of three. I took any job I could find. A year later, I got the good-paying job opportunity of managing Evergreen Lodge Rest Home."

"Yeah? I know all this. So?"

"Steve, life unfolds day by day. You will find the right job for you. Probably not tonight, but I know there are opportunities out there for you."

Steve took a deep, sighing breath.

"Right now, tonight, you need to tell Marge. Discuss your

options with her."

Steve stood up and dusted off the sawdust stuck to his jeans. "You're right. I should go home."

"Take the rest of the six-pack with you."

"I just had to let you know first." He walked away to his pickup.

I'm glad you did, she thought as she watched him drive away. *This is their problem. I won't meddle.* She prayed for Steve to be open and honest with Marge and for them to find their solution.

The sun sent finger shadows across her garden. Ethel sat lost in her thoughts as she remembered how she arrived on the coast.

After graduating from high school, she got a scholarship to the nursing school at the Vancouver General Hospital. She finished at the top of her class with a degree as a registered nurse.

The Veterans Administration hospital offered her a job. Ethel became the administrator of the nursing staff in a matter of a year. The new placement excited her, and her life centered on her job.

She visited the wounded soldiers on her daily rounds. One, Ian O'Rourke, caught her eye. Ethel and Ian talked daily. His recovery from shrapnel wounds had been lengthy. He told her he looked forward to his discharge.

One day, Ian held out a ring made from a pipe cleaner. "Will ye marry me?" he asked.

Ethel knew the protocol. All soldiers fell in love with their nurses. But. Did all nurses fall for the soldier?

She had.

She said yes. They planned to marry when he got

discharged from the hospital.

Ian had a job waiting with the Vancouver Fire Department after he left the hospital because of his military assignment in the bomb and fire detachment. His military experience impressed the Vancouver Fire Department.

“They look for guys like me,” Ian had said. “When my military discharge comes through, I've a job with the fire department and you can keep yours here at the hospital.”

They married the day Ian walked out of the hospital. They set up housekeeping in her tiny apartment.

In time, Ian's superiors noticed his ability in handling hazardous jobs. While working in Vancouver, a vacancy opened in the Coastal Fire Service. Ian applied, and they offered him the job.

“It's just what I want,” he told her. “I lived on the prairies and loved the country, but I'd like to try living near the ocean.”

“It means returning to my hometown and all my old friends. I think you should take the job.” she had answered.

He did.

The headquarters of the Coastal Fire Service was in Sechelt. Ian was supervisor of the various small volunteer fire departments from Egmont to Langdale.

Ian and Ethel found a cottage with a garden and soon started a family.

Coming back to the present, Ethel got up and wandered through her flower garden. Even as a small child, Steve enjoyed helping her in the garden. Now he maintained it for her. She loved watering and talking to the flowers.

Ethel stepped out of the garden, leaving the past behind.

She walked up her porch steps and looked around. As twilight set in, the sky was golden yellow to deep maroon and dark blue, she felt the chill. She sighed. *I best go inside*, she thought.

She entered the dark living room after securing her front door. Standing alone in the silent house, full of tidy knick-knacks, she tried to think.

Because she was the only occupant, her house stayed tidy. But her things got dusty. She got her dust-cloth and started dusting.

It was her way of clearing her mind to think.

Should I call Marge and warn her?

No!

Maybe I could call, say Steve is on his way home.

No!

Oh, what can I do?

She dusted another shelf.

Knowing there would be consequences, she had to call Marge.

This is not wise, she scolded herself as she lifted the phone receiver.

"Marge?"

"Hello, Ethel."

"Here's the problem...." She told Marge Steve's problem in four words and restrained herself from offering suggestions.

Marge took the news with a sigh. "Thanks for the warning." She did not sound thankful.

They hung up.

Ethel knew Marge was a positive person. When Steve got home, Marge would have some good ideas for him.

But she had a knot in her stomach. *How does Marge feel knowing Steve stopped here first? I hope I'm not in trouble.* She rearranged and dusted the knick-knacks again.

Chapter Three

Ethel spent a few days in her office at Evergreen Lodge, catching up on the paperwork that covered her desk. Work distracted her from the communication she had not received. She hoped Steve talked to Marge.

She leaned back in her chair, her desktop clean, every bill paid, all correspondence filed away. Open books on her desk got closed. The pencils and pens found their drawer. Ethel looked at today's activities on the desk calendar. The children played at the Lodge today. Ethel checked her watch as she waited for the doorbell to ring. When it did, she hurried down the long, carpeted hallway. It opened into a sunlit sitting room filled with quiet residents.

She opened the door to Steve and the children, all standing in a row. Ethel gave Jennifer a big hug as they came in.

Bobby squirmed out of her reach.

“Bobby, the games are by the fireplace,” she said.

He ran to the fireplace, saying hi to a resident.

Jennifer, being older, walked to the puzzles and chose one.

Steve had never brought the children before. He stood in the doorway.

"I guess you have spare time now to be with the kids," Ethel said. "Thanks for bringing them for their playtime with the residents. The old people look forward to their weekly visit. Don't just stand there. Come in."

She led him into the dining area next to the sitting room. They chose a table near the counter holding the coffee machine.

Ethel asked, "Coffee?"

"Sure," he said.

They kept coffee ready for residents and visitors. Ethel brought steaming mugs to their table.

She sat, leaning forward, ready to listen to Steve's story.

"I told Marge as soon as I got in the door. It didn't surprise her. Marge wants me to start my own cabinetry shop in our shed."

"That sounds like a good idea. You're very good at woodworking."

"I could, but it would take start-up money we don't have. Marge's idea is that we can live off her salary, and I can watch the kids while she works. You know me, Mom; I love my kids, but I'm not the guy who can be a stay-at-home dad. I would go nuts."

Ethel nodded. *Steve is not a guy to sit at the house for five minutes. He is too much like his dad. He needed to be part of the action.*

"I need a job that will make me money to set up a shop with the tools necessary. With start-up funds, Marge can help develop a client base. It'll work. There isn't a good cabinet shop on the coast."

"That's the truth. I've tried to get my kitchen cabinets

repaired for a year. So, I can be your first client. I never told you about the cabinets because you've been too busy logging."

"I need a job now!" Steve raised his voice and hit the table with his fist to make his point.

"Yes, a job with good pay." Her eyes wandered around the room to make sure Steve's outburst had not disturbed the residents. The morning papers littered a nearby table. The headline, Athabasca Mines in Alberta, caught her attention. She reached over and got it to read the story aloud.

Steve grabbed it out of her hands and kept on reading. When he finished, he looked at Ethel. "What do you think?"

Ethel said, "I have a second cousin that lives in the Fort McMurray area and works in that mine. I guess you could investigate that as an option."

Her words got Steve up and striding down the hall to her office.

Ethel followed.

Steve stood in front of her desk with the contact information in his hand. "I'll call the mine office now," he said as he dialed the phone.

Ethel nodded and sat at her desk to listen to his part of the conversation.

"Hi? Hello?" He paused. "Yes, I'm calling about a job with the mines." He paused. "Yes, I have blaster experience. I've worked sixteen years as a logger, and I've blasted stumps." He listened again. "Yes, I'll scan my resume right away." He looked at Ethel.

She opened her desk computer.

"Okay, great," he said into the phone. "What's blasters' pay?"

He paused. "Sounds good. When do you need me there?"
Steve smiled. "Next week? Fantastic! I'll get my information scanned for you within a few minutes. I'm looking forward to working for you."

Steve hung up the phone and turned to his mom. "Well, I have a job as soon as I complete the paperwork. It's a six-month contract as a blaster."

"That was fast," said Ethel.

"I want the job and they need blasters. Do you have the phone number for the bus station?"

"Yes, the bus schedule is in my filing cabinet. The file with your resume is on my computer under your name. You can update and scan it."

She relaxed and smiled. *Steve will have the bankroll to start his own business in six months. All he needs is Marge's approval!*

Steve sat at the computer updating his information. "I must convince Marge that I'll do this hard hat job. Monday I can start work. The pay is great!"

Ethel wondered if the 'hard hat job' meant convincing Marge or blasting in the mines.

"I'm ready to leave today!" he said as he copied and scanned his resume to the mine's office.

Ethel found Will's contact information. She wrote the bus schedule and Will's information on a slip of paper and handed it to Steve. She saw how anxious he was to get home.

Steve thanked her and left the office. He retraced his way to the sitting room, where the children played near the fireplace.

Ethel followed him again.

Steve got the children's attention when he said forcefully, □ "Time to go, Bobby and Jennifer. Say goodbye to your friends."

Jennifer whined. "But I'm not ready to go."

Steve gripped their hands and led them, protesting, to the door.

"Tell your grandmother goodbye. We gotta get home."

The excitement and energy the children brought left with them, returning the sitting room to a quiet space filled with canes, walkers, and wheelchairs. Logs crackled, and the flames danced in the fireplace lent the only activity to the room. The elderly folks loved it when the children came to play.

As she straightened up the games and gathered the loose puzzles, Ethel smiled at an elderly lady. "Jennifer and Bobby will be back next week. Their dad had an emergency today."

She left the sitting room and walked to her office.

Ethel thought *I would like to make a call to Will. Here I go again, meddling, putting my nose in where it doesn't belong. Steve can do this himself without my help. He's a grown man. Why do I try to help when it's not needed?*

She shrugged her shoulders and dialed the phone.

A man answered.

"Hi Will, this is your Aunt Ethel from B.C. I've a question for you."

Chapter Four

News travels fast around the Sunshine Coast. Soon, handwritten signs popped up all over town: Work Wanted.

Ethel wondered if Steve had posted any. She had not seen one with his name. But neither Steve nor Marge called her to say if he planned to leave over the upcoming weekend. He would have to get going if he was to be at the job site by Monday.

She picked up the phone to call Marge. She hesitated, then put the phone down. *Maybe I screwed things up enough they don't want to talk to me. I'll wait and see.* She sighed. *I'd better go pick Jennifer and Bobby up from school.*

It was Ethel's scheduled day to chauffeur the grandchildren.

As she drove near the school, she noticed her usual parking spot was open. She was early, but she did not want to take a chance of arriving after they got out of class.

Waiting always gave her too much time for memories. There was a space between her mind and the playground's jungle gym that held her thoughts.

Ethel wished she did not remember the night Ian answered the phone. The ringing had woken her from a sound sleep. She listened to Ian's side of the conversation.

"Hello?" he had said. "Okay. I'll meet you guys there. Call the paramedics."

Ian hung up and bolted out of bed. He dressed in a hurry. Before he left their bedroom, he leaned over and blew a kiss across her cheek.

She remembered hearing the front door close, the car's motor, and then the quiet. She had laid in bed, unable to go back to sleep.

Always, when the fire alarms sounded, it woke firefighters and their families.

She had gotten out of bed, put her housecoat on over her nightie, and wandered into her kitchen to make a cup of coffee.

The house had been so quiet that when she put the mug on the tile counter, it startled her.

One cup turned into two.

How long had she waited?

She no longer remembered.

An unrecognizable engine, not their vehicle, stopped in front of her house.

She remembered wondering why Ian took so long getting home.

Ethel hated this part of her memories. A person does not get over the pain of losing someone they love. Ian's death happened fourteen years ago, but she remembered it as if it were yesterday.

A disheveled firefighter came to her door.

"Ian's in the hospital. There was an a-a-accident at the fire." He had stuttered.

"An accident? What happened to Ian?"

"We heard a dog barking from inside of the residence. Even though it was completely engulfed in flames, Ian went in to rescue it. The ceiling collapsed on top of him." The firefighter stopped talking and looked at Ethel.

Her knees buckled.

He reached out to hold her upright.

She regained her composure to ask, "How bad is he hurt?"

The man whispered, "He's in the hospital's morgue."

"The morgue!" Ethel screamed. "No! Not Ian!"

She had grabbed her handbag. Forgetting her shoes, she ran across the lawn to the hospital's emergency entrance, in her slippers.

Inside, her nurse's training came back full force.

"Take me to him," she said with authority to the night duty doctor.

The rest of her memory blurred.

She sighed. *I want to remember the good times with Ian. Not this.*

As she reminisced, a pickup parked next to her. She had not been aware of it pulling into the lot.

Staring blankly, she did not see Steve wave at her through his window.

He got out, walked over to her car, and knocked on her window.

"Hey, Mom?"

She jumped and glanced at him as she returned to the present. Ethel blew her nose on the hankie she carried in her purse. Then she rolled down her window.

“Hi, son. What are you doing here? Why are you all dressed up? What's up?”

Steve wore a jacket, a button-up shirt, and clean jeans. Not his usual old jeans and a t-shirt attire.

“I'm catching the bus to Vancouver today. Then over to Alberta. I knew you'd be here waiting for the kids, so I came to talk to you.”

“Is Marge okay with you going?”

“It's not what Marge wants, but it's what I need. This opportunity is perfect for me.”

“How did the conversation go the other night?”

“When I got home that evening, we talked for a long time. Marge seemed tuned into the problem. We discussed the cabinet shop. The coast has no jobs for me. Marge knows that. She doesn't want me to go. But I'm going.”

“Okay. If you're sure. Where will you stay?”

“I called Will. He agreed to rent a room to me.”

“How much will he charge you?”

“He's asking a lot, I think. But what can I do? There are so many men flocking to that area for work that housing is at a premium.”

“Maybe you can make a deal with him. You only need a place to sleep.” She shrugged. She forgot Will was a scammer.

“I told Marge, it's only a six-month contract. It'll be over in a flash. Then I'll have the money to start my business. She will be my business partner and do the books.”

“Sounds good. I pray you can pull this off.”

"When I left, Marge was crying. But she understood my reasons for going. I gave her tooth fairy money for Bobby; in case one gets loose and falls out before I get home. He's of that age already."

Ethel thought *once he decides something, it' was a waste of time trying to change his mind.*

"I'll be back soon. Don't worry, Mom. Time flies. I've my suitcase, backpack, and a duffle full of tools. I'm ready to go."

Ethel wiped her eyes and said, "I know, kiddo."

"Cut and run. I can only leave that way. May I keep my pickup and keys at your house?"

Ethel nodded. She could barely speak. "Yes, of course."

Jennifer and Bobby ran up to the vehicles.

Steve gave each of his children big hugs and kisses as he told them goodbye. He bent down and planted a kiss on Ethel's cheek.

Then he got into his pickup and drove off.

Leaving them there.

Ethel wondered, *what have I done?* She was worried about Marge. Her daughter-in-law would have all the household responsibilities plus her job.

Ethel determined she would help Marge more than ever while Steve was away.

Chapter 5

Life between the two women settled into a workable situation.

Marge worked overtime at her job as much as she could to make up for the income loss.

Ethel commuted between the Lodge and Marge's house four afternoons a week.

Marge asked Ethel to sleep over three nights a week. It was much easier than commuting. It also seemed Marge wanted her company.

Ethel needed to be at the Lodge on weekends. Visitors came to visit their families. The folks looked forward to visits. Ethel's work doubled or tripled. Families wanted special things for their elderly parents. By Monday, her desk was clean, notes answered, bills paid. She went home happy, looking forward to Tuesday at Marge's. She wanted Marge as a friend, not just a relative.

Marge had weekends for herself and the children. They read books down by the bay, ordered pizza, or did nothing. She left the laundry for Ethel's return.

It took both women to keep the house and care for the children and work their jobs.

Today, when Ethel returned from Sechelt, she found Marge standing by the kitchen stove.

As she put her purse on the table, she said, "It's good to be back." She saw tears on Marge's face. "How was your day?" Ethel asked as she handed her a tissue from her purse.

Marge took it and blew her nose.

"Mine was full of problems," Ethel said. "I need to sit and relax for a minute."

Marge answered, "I'm worn out, too. Let's have some coffee."

Ethel appreciated Marge's effort at friendship. She nodded and sat down at the table.

Marge poured the coffee and joined her at the table.

"Thanks for the tissue. My sleeve was wet from crying. It's hard to get used to being alone after twelve years together."

"I found that out myself when Ian died." Ethel confided.

Q came out of wherever she had been and jumped on Ethel's lap. Idly, Ethel began to pet the cat.

Marge nodded in agreement. "Even if there was work here, Steve had his mind set. He has a place to stay, and he sends me a check each week. I must get used to him not coming home every night."

Ethel nodded without ever stopping stroking Q.

Marge had never opened up about her feelings. She hid behind the proverbial stiff upper lip, sucking in all her emotions. She was a trooper marching on. Steve's imminent return seemed to have opened Marge's emotional floodgates.

“He had already decided when he told me about the job and wouldn't change his mind.”□

Ethel said, sensing her misery, “It looks like everything has worked out, except getting into a cold, empty bed.” She saw the sadness in Marge's eyes, which parroted her own.

Marge said, “He kissed me goodbye and held me close in his arms. Whispering in my ear, 'I already miss you. I can't wait to come home'.”

I'll never forget the feeling of Ian's kisses, Ethel thought. *It's a magical memory.*

Marge peered out the window and went on. “He said, 'I'll be back before Jennifer's birthday.' He gave me a coin for Bobby's tooth fairy gift. Now, he's called and told me his boss, Ken, has offered him a supervisory position if he comes back! I don't know if I can handle much more time without him.”

Ethel wanted to hug her, but there was that wall between them. “Marge, I want to help you. I'll always be here for you. No matter what. You can trust me to do anything you need.”

She squeezed Marge's hand to reinforce her desire to be a part of Marge's life. “You're not used to having the responsibility of a family alone. Being a mom is difficult. Being a mom and a dad is harder. I know this, too."

Then, Ethel changed the subject as they approached territory they had never broached before in sharing their personal feelings. She shooed Q off her lap and picked up Bobby's backpack and put it by the door.

"This is ready for school. Has Jennifer finished her homework? She has a big assignment in science due Wednesday."

"She finished it. At least, it looks done to me." Marge said.

Bobby came into the kitchen. "What's for dinner?"

Q meowed.

"Q wants to know, too."

Marge reached down and ruffled his hair and said, "Slimy eels, fish guts, and lots of broccoli."

"Ew! I hope Q likes it! Can I go outside to play?"

Ethel nodded. "Yes, you may."

The children knew their grandmother was in control of homework and playtime. Their mom oversaw everything else. The women worked together to make life run smoothly at the O'Rourke home.

Bobby left Marge and Ethel sitting at the table.

Ethel loved her grandfather's handmade table. It had been hers until she gave it to Steve and Marge as a wedding gift. It was the focal point for large family dinners, books, notes, candy, hopes and dreams, and many conversations.

Marge looked around to see if anyone listened and pulled her chair closer to Ethel. She whispered. “Steve called this afternoon. He's coming home on Saturday.”

“That's great news,” Ethel whispered back.

“He said the bus connections are uncertain. He might be late. We're not to wait up for him.”

“Why are we whispering?”

“Steve wants to surprise the children.”

Ethel heard Jennifer's door open and wondered if her granddaughter had heard the whispered conversation. If she had, there would be questions.

Jennifer had not heard their discussion. She said, “I'm done with my homework. Can I go to the pier?”

Ethel answered, “Yes, you may. Please put your backpack beside Bobby's.”

Marge said, “Dinner's in two hours. Be back in time.”

Jennifer disappeared out the door and down the trail.

Ethel looked back at Marge and said, “Steve called me, too. He asked me to get his truck ready to go. His idea is to drop me off at my house and hurry home. He’s eager to get home to you.”

Marge raised her eyebrow as Ethel told her about Steve's conversation. Marge's expression was obvious to Ethel; she was both delighted Steve was in a hurry to get home and disappointed he would see his mother first.

“He said he wanted to hurry home? He won’t visit with you for a couple of hours first?” Marge asked.

Ethel nodded her head. “That is correct. He misses you as much as you miss him. I'll visit with him on Sunday. The six-month exile is over.”

Chapter Six

Marge had a standing invitation for Cap't Rolly and Ethel to come for dinner on Friday nights. Fun and games kept the children up very late.

Bobby's eyes drooped.

Marge said, "It's time for bed."

The children headed to bed with hugs and kisses. They made two trips around the table, getting goodnight kisses from Ethel and Marge, and hugs from Cap't Rolly.

"Growing like a weed," Cap't Rolly said after Bobby made his last round.

"He looks like a weed, too," Ethel said. "What happened to your knee, Bobby?"

Bobby lifted his shoulders in an I-don't-know gesture.

Ethel kissed his clean face, patted his backside, and sent him skipping off to bed.

"Bobby, the tooth fairy won't come if you don't go to bed," Marge scolded. Even though the tooth was not loose, yet.

With those words, the children left the kitchen, followed by Marge and Q.

Q slept with Bobby until it was night mouse hunting time.

An evening's boisterous energy slipped into quiet conversations between the three adults expecting Steve's return.

Ethel brought coffee and cookies to the table.

Cap't Rolly broke the silence. "It's fun filling in for Steve. Bobby, Steve, and I can go fishing before I find a new anchorage."

"That's a good idea," Ethel said. "No one stays in Secret Cove for the winter. It's been great having you around this summer. But I understand it's about time for you to leave. The best anchorage is in Horseshoe Bay Marina or Bowen Island Marina, across Howe Sound."

"We'll be sad to see you leave," Marge said. "Maybe you'll come back next spring?"

"I'm not making any plans. I'm looking for new adventures."

The conversation got around to the topic of Steve.

Marge said. "I remember our first date. Steve was my guy; I knew it right away. I was in love."

"I remember how Steve acted. He mooned around the house for days. His mind was someplace else." Ethel said.

They smiled at their memories.

"Our families lived in Sechelt. When we got married, I didn't want to live near any parents. I wanted to be on our own, with no help. This house in Secret Cove twenty-five minutes away was perfect."

Ethel said, "We hoped you would live in Sechelt. When your parents moved to Okanagan Lake, that left me alone in Sechelt."

Ethel winked at Marge. She looked at Cap't Rolly and watched him pull out his pipe. *Sucking on an empty pipe, holding a cup of coffee, or dusting were props to aid the thinking process.*

He closed his eyes, crossed his legs, and leaned back in his chair.

Marge said, "I'm curious. I knew little of your story. I'm interested to know how you came to our cove."

Ethel thought *he might feel edgy, telling his stories. But he seemed comfortable talking about himself when I asked.*

"I arrived in this cove shortly before Steve left," he said with his eyes closed. "Your Jennifer greeted me and became a friend from the first minute she saw me."

He opened his eyes and looked at Marge. "It's hard to let someone you love leave."

"What do you mean? I thought you told us your wife died?"

"You're right, Gracie died. Her death left me alone. Then I left Australia. My Tahiti Ketch is called *Grace*. The full name is *Amazing Grace*. Gracie, my wife, was amazing."

"I get it. Your boat is *Grace*. You sleep in her arms every night."

"That's it. She's my cradle where I rock to sleep with my memories every night. I sailed from Australia to Hawaii, then onto the coast of the United States mainland. I ended up here in British Colombia and found Halfmoon Bay and Secret Cove. A great place to anchor." He smiled.

"How long did it take to sail here?" Marge asked.

"I had no plans. I sailed where the wind took me. After meeting Jennifer, Bobby, and you, Ethel, and being invited to dinner at here, I decided to stay until the weather changed."

"So not just a re-provisioning stopover like other ports?"

Ethel asked.

"No, you folks made it impossible for me to leave." He grinned.

Ethel kept the rest of his story to herself.

He had told Ethel he never worried about anything besides his job. When Gracie passed away, he tried to cover his sorrow by overworking.

"Gracie and I lived aboard my thirty-foot ketch since we got married. She hid the leukemia from me until it caught up with her. Then she died and left me behind."

Ethel thought, *I know how it was for you. I experienced the same thing when Ian died. Steve was my only reason to live.*

Marge asked, "What made you want to live?"

"I didn't. I left Australia and sailed until I came to the Hawaiian Islands. My boat, bedraggled with torn sails and a broken spar, was a complete mess. Those months of trying to stay alive in severe storms made me realize, I didn't really want to die. I wanted to live."

"What did you do?"

"I repaired my boat. Cleaned myself up and had a fantastic dinner onshore, with ice cream for dessert. Then, I left Hawaii and headed for the United States mainland ready for adventure. Here I am, crabbing and selling my catch."

Ethel said, "Like when we met you on the pier."

"Yes, with my small rental cabin, I have one foot on land and one foot on the boat. The best of both worlds." He stood. Put his pipe in his pocket. "It's time for me to walk to my cabin. It's late for a crab catcher."

“Goodnight,” Marge said. “Thank you for sharing your story.”

Ethel said, “Good sleep. See you tomorrow.”

Cap’t Rolly walked away.

Ethel stood in the open door listening to his footsteps crunch along the dark path, then fade into silence. She listened to the night noises; tree branches blowing in the breeze, a car motor on the highway, a bear crashing through the forest, a dog barking at a shadow. She closed the door and turned to watch Marge finish cleaning up the kitchen.

Ethel gathered her knitting, and said, “Thanks, Marge. It was a fun evening again. I’ll leave early in the morning. I'm too tired to drive tonight.” She disliked going to her empty house, anyway.

“I really enjoyed hearing Cap’t Rolly’s story. Now I know a little more about our friend.” Marge yawned. “I’m tired, too. I’ll see you on Tuesday.” She went toward her room.

Ethel went to the bedroom Marge had given her. She was tired, not sleepy. Tomorrow could not get here fast enough. She missed Steve as much as Marge did.

Chapter 7

Ethel drove to town early Saturday morning. As she backed out, Marge stopped her and said, "I'm so anxious, can't work. I'll go shopping at the mall with the children. It's all I can do."

Ethel said, "That sounds like a good idea."

She drove away. Ethel had overheard Marge's plans for Steve's homecoming dinner. It did not include her. Their friendship was not a part of Marge's marriage. The children would tell her everything. She could wait.

She parked beside Steve's dusty pickup. It was six months since she put his keys in the entry table drawer. She switched them to her purse. He wanted her to check his truck so he could drive it home.

Ethel dressed for work and walked to the Lodge. Notes and bills littered her office desk. By six o'clock, her desk was clean, all the problems solved. The staff had the list of visitors for tomorrow.

"That's all for today," Ethel said to her staff in general. "You know where I am if you need me."

An orderly responded, "Affirmative."

Ethel walked home.

The unappetizing frozen dinner uneaten for six months got put in the microwave. Ethel missed the children's noises and Marge's conversations at dinner.

The phone rang as she ate.

It was Steve.

"I'm on the last ferry. I want to go straight home. I'll visit with you tomorrow, not tonight."

"Fine, I can wait. I would rather talk to you tomorrow, anyway."

"Mom, please meet me at the bus station in Gibbons. I want to drive straight to Secret Cove tonight. I'm ready to get home."

"You know I will."

"Thanks."

She hung up her antique phone thinking, *for me, tomorrow came tonight.* Talking to Steve about his plan for the homecoming satisfied her.

The 10 o'clock news was on when the phone rang again.

It was Steve, with a change in plans.

"Sorry. Change of plans. I'll call you when I reach the landing in Gibsons. I'll walk. Sitting for so long made me want to stretch my legs."

"Okay. I hope I can stay awake until then. I'll find a movie."

"Please drive my pickup to the pier. I'll drop you off at the Lodge and head for home. We'll get about five minutes to visit, but I am so tired I can hardly speak. I know it'll be late, but late is better than never. Right?"

She hung up and shook her head. “Why does he want to walk the two miles into Gibsons from the Ferry?” she asked the television.

Ethel settled back into her overstuffed recliner and promptly fell asleep.

The doorbell's persistent ringing woke her up.

She sat, wiped the sleep off of her face, straightened her hair, shuffled to the door in her slippers. As she shuffled to the door, Ethel thought *Steve would call from Gibsons. Who visits at this time of night? It's one o'clock in the morning.*

"Who is it?"

"It's Dr. Youst. I need to talk to you."

She opened to see Dr. Youst from St. Mary's Hospital. Ethel saw from the look on his face that he was uncomfortable. She knew him well as she was his head nurse for years until she took the administration position at the Lodge.

"It's late. Why are you here? What's happened?" She could see he stalled for words. *Just stay calm,* she thought. *What he wants to tell me will come out. He hasn't forgotten that I was his head nurse. I made him nervous back then, too.* "Don't keep me standing here. I'm waiting for Steve's call."

"Ethel, the RMPC brought in an accident victim an hour ago." There was a long pause. "It was your son, Steve." He looked away from Ethel and looked up at the ceiling as if to ask God for help.

Like a cold slap in the face, she was now wide awake. She felt the color washed out of her face. Her expression stiffened. Her lip quivered. "What happened? Where? How?" she asked questions without waiting for answers.

"I don't know." A puzzled look crossed his face.

Ethel collapsed in a chair near the door, digesting his words.

They were the wrong words. More wrong words came next.

In a soft voice, Dr. Youst said, “Ethel, Steve’s dead.”

“He’s what?” She looked up at him in a daze.

“He's dead.”

She screamed, “It can’t be true! How can this happen?”

“I'm so sorry, Ethel, but it’s true.”

Ethel realized that the doctor would come to her house in the middle of the night to tell her a terrible lie.

She repeated her questions. This time she wailed them loudly, so loud her staff at the Lodge next door came running.

Dr. Youst put his arm out for Ethel to take.

She stood facing him, ramrod stiff, her fists clenched at her side. Her eyes were bright with pain and disbelief. Trained as an emergency nurse, she could separate facts from her emotion...for a while.

“What happened?”

“I don't know.”

"Why don't you know? How come you don't know?" 'I don't know' was not the answer she needed.

Grabbing her coat, she stomped out of the house, elbowing past the doctor.

Without looking back, she crossed the lawn to the hospital. Her slippers fell off. She shoved the emergency doors open violently. She entered the darkened room, hitting the light switch with a vengeance.

Stark blue light flooded the empty room.

“Where is he?” she yelled.

Dr. Youst and the orderly from the Lodge followed her.

She stood in the middle of the empty room, looking around.

A doctor came through the doors to the emergency room examination rooms.

"Where is he?" she wailed, again. "Where is he? I want to see him!"

Ethel's screams alerted the officer in the RCMP station across the street.

A young duty officer came over. He stood watching for any signs of violence.

A group of hospital personnel stood by silently.

Ethel never raised her voice. She was always calm and polite.

□ Ethel yelled again, “Where is he?”

The ER doctor grabbed Ethel's arm and lead her to the cold storage door. He unlocked it. Then he wheeled Steve's body out and gently turned back the sheet.

Ethel gasped. "Oh no, no. He’s too blue."

He stood by the body and said, "Ethel, it's okay. It’s okay.” The doctor tried but failed to calm Ethel down.

Ethel screamed again. "No!" She touched Steve's hair, forehead, and patted his cheek. “No! no!” she spoke more softly.

Leaning over his body, she said, “It's not time for you to die. I am supposed to die first.”

She lay her cheek next to his face. "My baby’s so cold."

Dr. Youst and the RMCP officer entered the examining room. They, with the ER doctor, watched as she examined Steve. She lifted his arm. It was getting stiff. She stroked his head; a handful of hair came out in her palm.

Ethel, realizing her surroundings, did what nurses train to do. She made sure Steve was dead. His lack of vitals proved it.

She breathed more normally. She pulled the cold sheet over the blue body, and turned away, still holding the hank of hair in her hand.

Facing Dr. Youst, she asked, "Why can't you tell me what killed him?"

"I did the preliminary examination just as you did. There's nothing out of place." He responded, medical professional to medical professional.

“That's strange, hair keeps growing after death.” The ER doctor said as he looked at the hank of Steve's hair in Ethel's hand. "I saw nothing, either," he said, looking directly at Ethel.

"I don't either. No signs of violence. Not a mark on him. What now?" Ethel asked in her calm nurse voice. She tried to be practical.

Dr. Youst took a deep breath. "His body doesn't present any signs of violence or obvious trauma. It doesn't look like a heart attack or stroke. This death is highly unusual."

Ethel nodded. She could no longer speak.

“I’ll call the Medical Examiner in Vancouver to do an autopsy. That is the next step. Because it's Saturday night, it'll have to wait until Monday. But I'll call in the morning, anyway.”

The ER doctor returned Steve's body to the cold storage morgue.

Ethel let Dr. Youst guide her to a chair in the ER waiting room.

She sat, trying to understand what had happened to Steve.

She thought, *Steve's dead. Why am I acting this way? What's happening to me? I'm used to looking at bodies. The rest home has death often. I must pull myself together. Marge has to know, but I cannot call Marge acting like this.*

Ethel remembered their disagreements. Only one stood out. The job in Alberta. *Marge may blame me for Steve's death. That doesn't matter! What matters is letting Marge know! We waited all day for Steve to come home. Now, this! Marge needs me and I need her.* She took a deep breath.

"I'll talk to Marge calmly, like when one of our residents dies." She announced to the waiting Lodge orderly. She turned to Dr. Youst. "Where's there a phone I can use?"

"In there." The doctor pointed to the desk in the connecting hospital wing.

She went to wake Marge.

Ethel hung up the phone and marched back into the emergency room. She gave commands to the waiting RMPC officer. "Sir, take me to my daughter-in-law's house immediately. We need to talk to her officially. The mother-in-law is not the person to notify in this case."

In a determined voice, Ethel sent her employee back to Evergreen Lodge. "See that someone handles tomorrow's guests. I'll be at my son's house. Do your best. I don't want to worry about the Lodge."

She turned away so that they couldn't see her tears. *"Steve was my only son, my only child."*

Grabbing the officer's arm, she pulled him out of the door.

The orderly returned to the Lodge.

The officer wrenched his arm free of Ethel's grip. “I have to make a quick report at the station,” he said. “I'll tell them I'm going on the death notification and that I should be back in about two hours. Please wait for me."

Ethel waited in his car. She wrapped the hank of hair she held in her hand in her only unused tissue and tucked it in her purse.

During the twenty-five-minute drive, Ethel worried. *What would Marge do? Would she let me in her home? Should I stay with her and the children or go home? I can't be alone. The silence in my house is deafening.*

Then she remembered the children.

The children! Oh my!

Thoughts of her grandchildren brought fresh tears to her eyes and nose. She wiped her nose on her sleeve. Something she never did.

She decided she would spend the night with Marge.

The officer parked in Steve's driveway.

Ethel waited for the officer to collect his clipboard. Together, they walked to the door.

Ethel stood ramrod straight, her face colorless, lips tight, trying not to cry. She bottled all her emotions, took a deep breath, and knocked.

Chapter 8

As Ethel knocked on the door, she remembered she had always just walked into Steve's house. Somehow did not seem appropriate to do so now. But she opened the door, anyway.

"Marge?" she called softly.

"Steve?"

Ethel and the officer entered the kitchen.

Ethel went to Marge, who sat like a stone statue. She did not smile or cry. She just sat there, staring blankly. In her hands, she held the dishcloth she used to dry dishes.

The two women looked at each other. The same horrible grief registered on both faces.

The unavoidable truth sunk in as Ethel gathered Marge into her arms. Marge leaned on Ethel. Ethel leaned into Marge.

They both burst into tears.

We need each other, Ethel thought. *I cannot do this alone and neither can she.*

"What happened?" Marge asked between sobs. "You always have the answers to medical problems."

“No one knows anything,” Ethel whispered through her tears.

The noise woke the children. They both stumbled sleepily into the kitchen.

Ethel saw them standing in the doorway, watching. It took all her willpower to stop crying, go to them, and gather them in her arms.

She needed to tell them something. She knew Marge could not.

“Your daddy can't come home,” she said. She could say nothing else.

The children clung to her and started to cry as well.

Ethel was sure they did not understand why their mom and grandmother sobbed.

The forgotten officer stood waiting by the doorway.

Finally, with a sob, Marge looked up and saw him. “What happened?”

The officer opened his file and read his report of the night's events in a very analytical and non-emotional voice. Then he answered Marge's questions.

While he talked, Q wound herself around Ethel's legs as if to comfort the older woman. Ethel looked at the children. *Did they understand this?*

Their vocabulary did not include words such as death and dead until the officer gave the family his report. She saw Jennifer getting the idea.

When Marge ran out of questions, the officer closed the file and laid it on the table. “It is time for me to go. If you need anything further, here's my card.” He placed a business card on top of the file and left.

Ethel wondered if Jennifer remembered when her hamster died. They buried it, sang a song, and cried a few tears. *Jennifer will be in for questions when it all sinks in.*

Bobby was too young to remember the hamster.

She glanced at Bobby. He looked worried.

He said, with tears rolling down his cheeks, "I made my mommy cry. I want her to stop crying. What did I do?"

Ethel said, "No, sweetheart, you did not make your mom cry. You did nothing wrong." She hoped Bobby would not feel any responsibility for his dad's death. "Bobby, come here. I want to tell you something." She pulled him up onto her lap.

"Okay. But what's wrong?" he whimpered as he snuggled into her arms.

"Your daddy won't come home. Your mommy wanted to say hello to him. But she has to say goodbye. She didn't get what she wanted. When you get what you want, you're happy. If you don't, you're sad and you cry."

Her words worked. Bobby slid down off her lap and ran to hug his mother. "It's okay, Mom. I won't ever say goodbye."

Marge gave Bobby a hug and a weak smile. "You'd better not."

"Bedtime," Ethel said with authority.

"Good night, Mom," chorused the two bewildered children. They left the room with their grandmother in tow.

Ethel blew them kisses and left their doors open a crack, giving the darkened rooms a bright edge. Q curled up in her usual place of Bobby's bed.

Ethel returned to find Marge reading the accident report. She made a pot of coffee and watched Marge while the machine filled the pot. She brought steaming cups to the table and sat beside Marge. Stirring and sipping was something to do.

They looked at their cups instead of at each other. For the moment, the tears stopped. They say silently for several minutes, each with their own thoughts.

Ethel stated her thoughts out loud. “What shall we do?”

She got a blank stare from her daughter-in-law.

Marge was the proverbial deer caught in the headlights, frozen in place.

Ethel had a puzzle with no pieces or answers. She announced forcefully, “Until we have some answers, we cannot bury Steve.”

She knew Marge did not know what to do next.

Chapter Nine

The guard waved Ethel over to the visitors' parking lot.

She and Cap't Rolly planned to meet the funeral director at the hospital in Vancouver. It had been about all Ethel to do to ride the ferry across to the city. She needed Cap't Rolly's moral support. She wanted to talk to Dr. Lowe, the head pathologist, as soon as possible.

Walking into the hospital, they took the elevator down to the autopsy labs.

A junior pathologist met them in the hall. After clarifying that Ethel was the dead man's mother, he said, "We're conducting extensive internal testing. What happened to his head? He has a sizable bunch of hair missing. That's the only sign of foul play."

Ethel opened her purse and took out a tissue. She handed it to the pathologist. "I ran my fingers through his hair, and it came out in my hand."

"I'll sample some of the hair you got immediately after death. I'll compare it with the sample I already took.

Dr. Lowe joined them in the hall. He took Ethel's hand and said, "Ethel, I am so sorry for your loss. Please accept my condolences. My office is on the second floor. Let's go there to talk. You really shouldn't be down here at the autopsy rooms."

When Cap't Rolly took a step to follow, Dr Lowe said, “I'm sorry, and you are?”

“I'm the one who should apologize,” said Ethel. “Dr. Lowe, may I present Roland Robinson. He's a family friend.”

The men shook hands and greeted one another.

They rode up the elevator to the office.

Ethel felt glad they left the formaldehyde smell of death in the basement.

"What can you tell us?" said Cap't Rolly.

Dr. Lowe said, "It looks like accidental poisoning.”

“Accidental? How could he accidentally ingest poison?” Ethel could not wrap her head around that idea.

“I don't know the answer to that question. I'm sorry.”

“You're sure his death was because of poisoning?”

“Fairly positive. There were strong indications during the autopsy. It would be interesting to find the source of the poison. We'll have the contents of his stomach analyzed.”

“Okay. Well, thank you. Is that all you can tell me?”

“At this time, yes. The final determination will take place after we get the tox report.” He paused. “Now, if you haven't any more questions, I have some papers for you to take to the mortuary. And there is a release-of-body form for you to sign. As I said, the toxicology tests should be back in a week.”

Ethel signed and accepted the paperwork. When Dr. Lowe gave her Steve's belongings, there was only the backpack. *He must've left his other things in Alberta,* she thought. *I guess he decided to go back and take that supervisor job. Oh Steve, what will I do without you?*

Once she and Cap't Rolly were alone, she said, "I got one answer. I have more questions and no answers."

"Poison."

"Yes." She sighed. "You'll have to drive. I've had enough for today."

They met the transport van from the mortuary in Sechelt. Ethel arranged for Steve's body's cremation.

Ethel planned to spend the night with Marge.

When Cap't Rolly drove up to the house, Ethel noticed that there were already flowers down at the pier for Steve. She saw Patti walking up from the pier and knew the neighbor lady would stop by yet that evening. Probably to pick up her casserole dish, but really to check on Marge.

Cap't Rolly stayed for supper.

As they sat around the table, Marge said, "Eat anything on the table."

Ethel opened her mouth to say that there was no way they could eat all the casseroles from friends that crowded the table, but Jennifer interrupted her.

"Grandma, I want to put Dad in the ocean to become part of the world. He loved the fish and fishing."

"How do you plan to do this?" Ethel asked. She quickly glanced at Marge who seemed dazed.

"I want a gathering at the pier and some words and a prayer, like when my hamster died. Then we get on Cap't Rolly's boat and motor out to the divide between Thornaby and Merry Island and say goodbye to Dad."

"That's a good place to send him out to sea," said Cap't Rolly.

"It seems the right thing to do," Ethel agreed.

After dinner, Jennifer took charge of movie night. They all escaped reality by watching *Free Willie*. Tomorrow, they would set Steve free.

At eleven o'clock in the morning, they stood in a line on the porch, dressed and ready to walk down to the pier.

Ethel carried a bouquet of sorrel Jennifer gave her. She asked, "Jennifer, did you tie the flowers with your ribbon, one of your beautiful hair ribbons?"

Jennifer nodded.

They processed to the pier. Friends and neighbors were there to say goodbye to Steve.

His ashes were in a beautiful handmade wooden box. Marge held the box close to her chest.

Marge whispered to Ethel, "I won't say goodbye. I'll say, see ya later. But not here, in front of all these people. I'm not good at speeches." She stood there like a blank-eyed zombie at the pier.

When the service ended, the priest thanked and blessed those in attendance. Neighbors and friends hugged Marge and Ethel before wandering away.

Cap't Rolly signaled, and the children climbed aboard *Gracie*.

Jennifer carried a lovely bouquet from the pier.

Cap't Rolly helped Ethel climb on board. He held his hand to Marge, and she tried to get on the boat with the box in her arms.

"Here." She passed the box to Ethel.

Cap't Rolly then helped her board.

She sat beside Ethel and held out her hands to retrieve the box.

Ethel understood and handed the box back. She had given her boy away once before when they married.

Cap't Rolly started the engine and stowed the gear. "Jennifer, come up and throw off the dock lines," he ordered.

Gracie ran smoothly toward their destination, the divide between Merry Island and Thornaby Island.

Cap't Rolly found a suitable spot and set the anchor.

Marge handed him the box.

Capt. Rolly unscrewed the lid and handed Marge a beautiful white satin bag holding Steve's ashes.

Marge handed the bag to Ethel. "I can't pour his ashes into the sea. Please help me."

Ethel took the bag and held onto Marge. Ethel could not talk for crying. She saw a silent tear slid down Cap't. Rolly's cheek.

Jennifer and Bobby stood by Marge, and they all watched Ethel pour the contents into the sea. They watched the ashes float away.

Ethel said, sobbing as she handed the satin bag back to her. "Marge, do you want to say anything?"

Marge mumbled, "See ya later, alligator."

Jennifer and Bobby laughed one quick giggle. They always said that to their dad.

Ethel pointed to the bouquet sitting on a cushion.

Jennifer stepped up to the stern rail and gave the flowers a big toss. They landed amid the ashes. The flowers floated, pushed out of sight by the wind and waves.

Cap't Rolly cleared his throat and said, “Afternoons get rough, and the wind is up. We should head for calmer water in Secret Cove.”

Bobby sang, row, row your boat...

Everyone joined in and sang the ditty several times.

What a funeral, Ethel thought. *I won't forget this one ever!*

When the singing stopped, the talking began.

Jennifer stood at the stern, holding the rigging, facing them like a lawyer in charge of a trial. She asked, “What caused Dad to die?” Without waiting for an answer, she continued. “We know it was poison. There was no other problem, no heart attacks. Nothing else was wrong. But how? Why?”

Cap't. Rolly said, “We'll know more in another week.” He changed the subject. “Say, how would you all like to go fishing tomorrow since it's Saturday? If it's okay.”

The children said yes.

Ethel said, “Maybe.”

Marge said, “No.”

They returned to the dock.

Bobby was sound asleep.

“May I impose one more time?” Ethel asked Cap't Rolly as he tied to the dock.

“Sure, I'll pack this guy to the house. Maybe he will stay asleep."”

Cap't. Rolly deposited Bobby on his bed.

Ethel said, “Thanks.”

"That's okay. See you tomorrow to go fishing."

"I'm not sure I'll be there. I'm needed at the Lodge on the weekends."

After Cap't Rolly left, Ethel turned to her granddaughter. "Jennifer, you did a fantastic job sending your dad out to sea today. Would you like to stay up past your bedtime?"

"Thanks, Grandma. Yes!"

The three females collapsed around the kitchen table.

"How about a soda?" Ethel asked. She brought cookies with the soda to the table.

They drank and nibbled in silence.

Ethel started mulling over questions about Steve's death. Those questions haunted her. She thought *I've been at Marge's house long enough. I needed to go home. I need to deal with the Lodge.*

She rose, went to her room, stuffed her things into her small carry-on and knitting bag. Q wrapped herself around and around Ethel's legs while she packed.

"What do you think, cat? Will my broken heart ever mend? Do you think rubbing up against my legs will help?"

Q purred.

Ethel headed to the kitchen to say goodbye

Marge looked up at her. "Where are you going?"

"I'm in charge of Evergreen Lodge. They need to know they have a boss. I've been gone for a week. Now it's time to check-in, or they may fire me."

Jennifer said, "Will I see you tomorrow fishing?"

"It depends. I usually cannot get away from the Lodge on the weekends."

Marge said, "Count me out."

Ethel knew Marge needed some time to be alone. If she stayed, she would quickly become Marge's crutch. *Marge needs to reach out to me.* For once, she would not interfere.

Ethel drove to Evergreen Lodge. Everything was in place. She left a note for the head nurse that she would not be in on Saturday.

Coming into her home was usually pleasant, not tonight. She was exhausted. She knew she would find a house full of dust and dirty dishes.

Chapter Ten

Ethel woke with a start on Saturday morning. She grabbed coffee for the drive and went straight to the pier. Marge and the children waited for *Grace*.

It surprised Ethel to see Marge. “What happened?”

“Jennifer convinced me last night after you left. She reminded me that I loved fishing. She said I needed a good fishing trip with Bobby. Not a funeral, but a fishing trip.”

“Excellent decision.”

“I packed a lunch. And here I am. Why aren't you at the Lodge?”

“I decided they could get along without me one more day. I stopped by last night. They're holding down the fort just fine. I felt I needed to be with you.”

“I'm glad you're here. I didn't want to stay in the house alone."

“I certainly understand that one.”

When *Grace* docked, they all boarded.

Bobby found his seat on Capt. Rolly's lap so he could steer.

Two hours later, in Howe Sound, Cap't Rolly set his crab

traps.

The girls watched.

Cap't Rolly baited, lowered, and secured the traps, leaving an orange float sticking up to mark their place.

Bobby helped by getting in the way.

“I've set the traps. Tomorrow morning, I'll retrieve them, full of crabs,” said Cap't Rolly.

Grace drifted.

Cap't Rolly snagged a dead, bloated fish in his net. Then he snagged three more. He bagged them and looked them over.

Ethel saw him write a notation of the boat's location time of day when he bagged the fish.

The afternoon wind made the sea rougher.

Ethel said, “Is it okay if we troll to the cove?”

“Yes, good idea.” Cap't Rolly put *Grace* in gear and headed for the cove.

While Marge and the children packed in their poles, Ethel went to Cap't Rolly at the helm. She lowered her voice. The ka-thump of *Grace's* engine covered her words.

“What were you doing? I watched you with the fish. What's wrong with them?”

“Boy, you're observant. I thought I was sneaky.”

“You were. The children think they can outsmart me. I see everything. What gives?”

Cap't Rolly said, “I'll look at the fish and see what killed them.”

That statement bewildered Ethel.

“How would you do that?”

“I was the Director of The Marine Forensic Lab for the City of Sidney, Australia. I'm a marine biologist. It's a great job and too demanding. After Gracie died, I needed a break. I wanted to start fresh. So here I am.”

Two days later, Ethel went down to the pier to see Cap't Rolly. She was interested in his progress. Opening the door, she saw him standing over a microscope.

Jennifer sat silently on a stool, with her finger poised in the air.

Not wanting to interrupt, Ethel closed the door. *Later,* she thought. *When they finish for the day, I'll come back.* She walked to the house to spend time with Marge.

Evening came, Jennifer ran into the house to report her day.

Ethel walked to the rented cabin to hear what Cap't Rolly discovered.

They sat by his fire. Cap't Rolly lit his pipe and recapped the day for Ethel.

“My notebook held the specific details of the capture. I photographed and recorded notes on the first fish and each fish. I recorded and photographed each fish after an initial study of them. That was yesterday.”

Ethel interrupted his story. “She came into the house. Marge couldn't stop laughing. It was so good to hear her laugh again. She hasn't laughed since Steve died. She told Jennifer that you used to be a fish detective.”

He smiled around the stem of his pipe.

“Thanks for letting her be your assistant.”

“I have strict rules. Don't talk or interrupt, sit and do what I say. Jennifer obeyed. Her job is to hit the on and off buttons on my recorder. The scientific method excites her. I answered Jennifer's questions when we finished for the day. Her questions were all very scientific. She'll make an excellent scientist someday."

Ethel smiled, feeling proud of her granddaughter.

Cap't Rolly went on. "I discovered the same poison in all four fish. The water might be the problem. I need to report this to Dr. Lowe. It may be a different poison from what killed Steve. But it's too important to keep it to myself. Would you meet me at the marina tomorrow and drive me around Vancouver? It's getting late enough in the year. I need to berth *Grace* over there from now on."

"Sure, I'll pick you up."

Ethel took the first ferry over to Vancouver the following day. Riding the ferry was still difficult. She thought about Steve for the entire trip.

She picked up Cap't Rolly at the marina. They arrived early for their meeting with Dr. Lowe.

As they barged into his office, he said, "Ethel, Mr. Robinson, hello. What can I do for you?"

Cap't Rolly put a file on the doctor's desk. "My name is Dr. Robinson. My occupation was as Lead Marine Biologist with the Department of Fisheries in Sidney, Australia. Here are my credentials. Most people just call me Cap't Rolly."

Dr. Lowe leafed through the resume. "You're well qualified as a marine biologist. But that does not explain why you're here."

"Let me show you what I found. There may be a link between fish poisonings and Steve's death. A rare heavy metal called trillium poisoned the fish. Do you make any toxicology reports on poisoning in Vancouver? Can we check for poisoning by trillium?"

Dr. Lowe reached for his phone. "I need a toxicology report from all hospitals, clinics, and other medical group's records that mentioned this kind of poison."

While they waited for the return phone call, he and Cap't Rolly went over the findings.

Ethel sat on a chair and closed her eyes in silent prayer.

The results came back fast. Hospitals and clinics had reported a rash of trillium poisonings in the Horseshoe Bay area. Many people had come into various ERs with food poisoning.

The heavy metal trillium was an uncommon poison. It was odorless, colorless, tasteless, absorbed through the skin. It was impossible to buy. No one sold it.

Dr. Lowe said, "We got Steve's toxicology report back. He had ingested trillium. How he got this poison stumps us."

Ethel noted that none of the reported food poisonings resulted in death.

Dr. Lowe told them the reports showed that all victims contacted the poison in the North Shore area.

"What about the origin of the contaminant?" Ethel asked.

"As far as I know, they did not investigate any of the deaths. There are no police reports. There are no signs of foul play. All hospitals and clinics reported accidental poisoning."

They needed to go in different directions to trace the root of the poison. Dr. Lowe's job was people's deaths. Cap't Rolly's was oceanographic biology issues. Ethel's only concern was Steve's death.

She drove Cap't Rolly to the main offices of the Department

of Fish and Game. Then they went to the Department of Water and Power. And finally, to the Department of Highways.

At every stop, he talked, and Ethel listened to the managers of the various departments. There was a lot of interest in what he discovered.

Back in the car after the stop at the last government department, Cap't Rolly said, “I may have opened a can of worms.”

“It kind of looks like it from that construction guy's scowl.”

“A definitive answer is necessary, more proof, not supposition. I need the source of the contaminant. We found the fish in Howe Sound,” he said. “That area is where we need to return and look for the point of contamination.”

“They built the Highway in record time because of the Olympic games. Maybe the problem relates to blasting.”

“Can you show me around? I don't know this city, and I don't have a car.”

“I'll call the Lodge and clear my calendar. I can stay here in Vancouver tonight on one condition. Let me sleep on *Grace* instead of spending money on a hotel or ferry passage.”

“Sure, plenty of room for you. I'm hungry. Let's find a restaurant.”

Cap't Rolly's cell phone rang as they walked toward the restaurant they had chosen.

It was the construction boss contracted under the Department of Highways.

Ethel could hear the loud, gruff voice as he yelled through the phone.

“Hey, I got your message. What? You accuse us of

contaminating the ocean and killing fish? That makes us responsible now? We did our jobs just like they said. Don't make trouble, or you'll be sorry." The man hung up without waiting for Cap't Rolly's response.

Ethel said, "What did he mean?"

Cap't Rolly shrugged it off. "Just words. Spouting off steam."

The following day, Ethel drove Cap't Rolly up the North Shore Highway and parked beside a visible rubble deposit.

She watched while he climbed down the steep, slippery embankment, loaded with test tubes and baggies. The rocks moved and slipped as he scrambled down.

Cap't Rolly sampled the dead tide pools. He waded out to take a water sample. With his backpack filled, he scrambled up the rocks to the car. He was wet, dirty, and scratched up and a tear in his pants at the knee.

"Ethel, please drive to Dr. Lowe's office. The water may contain heavy metals. Trillium is part of the chemicals in blasting caps. The residue is washing out to sea."

Ethel drove Cap't Rolly to Dr. Lowe's office.

"I'll pass on your findings. Was it the road department's fault?" asked Dr. Lowe.

"It's too early to tell."

Dr. Lowe said. "If it is, the department will pass the buck. It may land in the laps of the contractors who bid on the jobs."
Cap't Rolly repeated the contractor's conversation and added, "The department approved the work."

After they left Dr. Lowe, Ethel asked, "What is next?"

"Do you know any protest groups that deal with the oceans?

I want to present the results to the biggest protest group," said Cap't Rolly.

"Yes, I do. Save Our Seas, also known as S.O.S. It's a sizable, active group. They get people involved. I'll help you find their phone number, but then I want to go home. I want to check on Marge."

"Okay. Thanks for all your help. I'll call a taxi."

She hated leaving Cap't Rolly, but it seemed he was off on a tangent now. Steve's death was her mission. Figuring out how he died was the only thing she wanted to do.

After a two-hour wait in line for the ferry, she got home. Rather than driving to Marge's, she drove home and called Marge.

Marge sounded tired, scattered, and basically fine. Patti was with her.

Ethel dusted her knick-knacks and thought about what to do. She decided to take a leave of absence from the Lodge until they solved Steve's death.

Returning home from the Lodge, she cooked a solitary dinner. As she finished washing dishes, the phone rang.

Cap't Rolly sounded exhausted, but animated.

"I met the S.O.S. group and gave a rundown on the contamination and the dead fish. It impressed them. They want to pressure the government."

"Good. It looks like you hit the right group," she said.

"Dr. Lowe called and invited me to a dinner meeting with the Health Department, the Fish and Game, and contractor of the Road Development representatives. I just got out of the meeting. The discussion concerned the cleanup. The consensus was that the cleanup the contractor's job. Everyone saw the contractor's anger. He left without a word."

"Didn't that scare you after the phone call you got last night?"

"It's just words. S.O.S. wants to target the construction company, and I am the construction company's target," said Cap't Rolly.

"What can they do to you?"

"We'll wait and see. I have a full schedule of meetings tomorrow."

"Do you need me?"

"Yes, please. I need a chauffeur. I'm headed to the marina and sleep. See you when you get here tomorrow."

"It's a deal. I'll take the first ferry and meet you at the *Grace* in the morning. Good night."

Chapter Eleven

Ethel knocked on the cabin and stepped onto the *Grace.*

A bedraggled, cut, and bruised Cap't Rolly slid back the hatch. He mumbled 'good morning' and motioned for her to come down into the cabin.

“What happened to you?” She handed him one cup of coffee she brought. Strong and black, it was just what she thought he needed.

“Had a long, rough night.” He nodded in gratitude for the coffee and took a sip.

“It looks like you fought the devil.”

Cap't Rolly sat on the settee and closed his eyes, as if trying to recapture the night before.

“It happened when I came home from that dinner that I called you about.”

“Yes, I remember you said you weren't worried about anything.”

“I was on the gangway when two men moved in and attacked me. I fought back.”

“I bet you were in fights when you were young. All boys do, it seems."

"I knocked one thug into the water. But his buddy caught a lucky shot on my chin. It was lights out for me." He took a sip of coffee. "When I came to, I was on the gangway between a dock box and the bow of a boat. I finally could stand and limp to the *Grace* and saw they violated her, too."

"What?"

"Look around." He waved his arm toward the mess. "They broke the hatch and the latch. You see the mess they made of my equipment. They left a note on the navigation table warning me to leave Canada."

"What did you do?"

"I called security. I was so mad, I yelled at them. They're supposed to keep outsiders off the docks."

After a gulp of coffee, he continued. "The RCMP came. They made a report, took pictures, and bagged the note for fingerprints. They told me to go to the clinic to get checked out. I rode with them. After a couple of hours in the clinic, I hitched a ride back to the *Grace*. I couldn't tell you how long it took or what time it was, but dawn wasn't far away."

"Any broken bones?" Ethel, always the nurse, asked.

"No."

"No wonder you were still asleep when I got here."

"I thought they might come back so I locked the hatch from the inside. I got my machete before I laid down on the settee to sleep."

"And I woke you up."

"You stepping on the boat made it rock. That woke me up."

"I'm glad you're still alive."

"What time is it?"

Ethel looked at her watch. "Time for lunch. I caught the 11 o'clock ferry over from Sechelt. Besides coffee, I brought us fish tacos." She handed him one.

He drained his coffee cup and put the taco aside. "Thank you. Where did you get the tacos?"

"Over there." She pointed to the dock and the path leading to the ferry terminal.

Cap't Rolly put his cup down and placed his taco in a baggie.

"What are you doing?"

"I'm taking it to the medical examiner's office."

"Well, if he's hungry, we can get him one. I ate one. It was good." Then she said, with a certain urgency, "I need to use your bathroom."

Cap't Rolly grabbed his keys and wallet. "Come," he said. "We're going to the hospital and get your stomach pumped."

"Why? That's unnecessary. I need to use your bathroom."

He pulled her up the gangway and shoved her into the backseat of her car. He tossed the bagged taco in with her.

"Where's the nearest hospital?"

She told him. Her voice slurred.

He drove to the emergency entrance and pulled her into the waiting room. With a loud voice, he got a doctor's attention.

Cap't Rolly made it very clear. "I want everything you pump out of her stomach bagged for me."

They rushed Ethel away.

An hour later, Cap't Rolly poked his head into the room.

Spying Ethel, he asked, “Are you okay?”

Ethel nodded.

The doctor in the room said, “You can come in. She's fine. She needs to rest for a few hours, but she should be ready to go home soon.”

Cap't Rolly nodded his thanks to the doctor and said to Ethel, “Do you want me to call Marge?”

Ethel shook her head and managed a strangled whisper. “No.”

She closed her eyes and listened to the hum of the machines and the men's voices.

“While Ethel's in the hospital, I'll go to the medical examiner’s lab with the contents of her stomach. In a few hours, we'll have the results.”

“I'll call Dr. Lowe and report what happened here. He might want to get in touch with the Health Department. Do you know where she got the fish?”

Later, Ethel drifted into semi-consciousness and heard them talking again.

Cap't Rolly said, “What's going on here? She was fine when I left a couple of hours ago.”

She heard the doctor say, “Ether's prognosis wasn't good. We had a code blue. Her urine was dark green. She had a critical, adverse reaction to the poison. It got into her bloodstream.”

“I know the antidote for trillium poisoning. I've researched this poison extensively.”

“I've never heard of this poison, let alone of an antidote.”

“It is crucial that you follow my instructions immediately! Call

Dr. Lowe if you don't believe me. If you don't do as I say, I will hold you responsible for her needless death. I won't forget. And neither will her daughter-in-law and grandkids."

Hours later, Ethel came out of the coma. She turned her head and smiled at Cap't Rolly, praying by her bedside.

He smiled in return. "Welcome back."

Words did not come. Her throat was too sore from the purge.

Cap't Rolly got up to leave and patted her on the head. "I'll be back."

As he walked out of her room, he whistled softly the tune Row, Row, Row Your Boat.

Chapter Twelve

Ethel opened her eyes and looked around. She was in an unfamiliar room and wondered how she got there. They had outfitted the room with all the things the hospital had for intensive care. Then she remembered the frantic trip to the hospital. Her memory was blank except for the vision she had of Steve. She closed her eyes and smiled, remembering the vision.

It was her call to action. In the vision, Steve was at peace. He pointed to his stomach and his mouth. He walked away, his face happy and serene.

That was all she remembered when she woke up. She would keep it to herself. No one would believe she saw Steve. It made perfect sense to her. She would share it with Marge later.

She opened her eyes again and saw a nurse fiddling with a machine.

“Why am I in the ICU?”

The nurse replied, “Do you remember being poisoned?”

Ethel nodded; her throat too sore to speak.

“The poison got into your bloodstream. You were in a coma and close to death.”

“I don't remember any of that,” she whispered. “I want to leave. I’m fine.” The words came out in a murmur.

“The doctor ordered bed rest. He said that we need to watch you one more day.”□She put a newspaper on the tray table.

Ethel saw her face on the front page.

Cap't Rolly leaked the story to the S.O.S. protest group. Her face was on all the television and newspapers as the poster child, or lady, helping to save Horseshoe Bay.□

Ethel hated the notoriety. This was not her campaign.

The connection between the dead fish and Steve's death was plain. She knew what killed Steve. *But why? Why did someone murder Steve?*

Ethel was ready to leave. She was not a patient, patient.

“I'm checking out. I'm fine. I'm leaving,” she firmly whispered.

She dressed, picked up her purse, and rode the elevator to the lobby. She saw no reason to wait until the nurse returned with a wheelchair – or worse, a doctor who would force her to stay.

There was a small crowd waiting to confront her outside the entrance.

She did not want to go back inside the hospital to call for a cab.

Arthur, the S.O.S. spokesperson, walked over and offered to take her to the ferry.

She gratefully accepted.

Waiting like a circling shark was the S.O.S. group’s special reporter. They made their way through the group and walked over to Arthur’s car.

Ethel settled into the back seat.

Arthur and a reporter got in the front seat.

The barrage of questions started once they pulled into the street.

Ethel did not answer any of the reporter's questions. “I'm not the issue. Cap't Rolly is the one who brought you this issue.”

Finally, they gave up and drove to the ferry in silence.

“Thanks for the lift. I appreciate your respect for my silence. You need to talk to Cap’t Rolly.” Ethel said with a smile.

Today, the dock had security. Ethel had to show her credentials before they let her in the marina gate.

She went to the *Grace* and knocked. No one answered. Turning to go, she spotted Cap't Rolly walking down the gangway.

Cap’t Rolly said, “Hey! You look okay. How do you feel?”

“I feel tired, but good. My throat can use a little rest. Thanks for all you did to save my life.” Ethel said with all her heart.

They walked to her car. She drove to the ferry lineup.

“How did you get here from the hospital?”

“Arthur from the S.O.S. and a reporter gave me a ride. They asked a lot of questions. You'll have to talk to them.”

He told her about the progress made with the Fish and Game Commission. “The S.O.S. group has a powerful lobby. I'll head up a study. It could take months. I'll stay on this side of Howe Sound until we get answers.”

They talked, sitting in her car, about all his plans. She said nothing of hers.

“The ferry's here. I'll leave you now,” said Ethel. “I can't wait to get back to Sechelt and call Marge. Thanks again for your help. You're a good friend. Goodbye.”

"See you later. I'll stay in touch during the winter. Take care."

He got out of her car with a little wave.

She waved back and drove onto the ferry.

On entering her house, she picked up the phone and called Marge. She was eager to go to Secret Cove.

Marge answered on the fifth ring, as usual.

"I'm home. I caught the noon ferry. Do you want me to pick up the children from school?" Ethel picked up a dust rag while Marge spoke. "Sure, I'll spend the night. I'll see you soon."

Ethel stopped and bought a Vancouver newspaper on her way to the school.

Parked in her usual spot, the children recognized her car and ran to get in. They talked all the way home. Ethel gave each a hug. They put their bags in the kitchen and went outside to play. Ethel hugged Marge, too. Q wrapped herself around Ethel's legs.

"Glad to be home. Vancouver is tiresome. How are you?" Ethel put the newspaper on the table.

Marge saw the front page and Ethel's face staring back at her. She quickly scanned the story. "How did you get involved with a group like S.O.S.?"

"I didn't. Cap't Rolly did."

Marge read the story and said, "Ethel, you're a real activist. I didn't know. You seem too old for that. You just worked at Evergreen Lodge, helped us, and knitted."

"There's a lot about me you don't know. I'll make myself some honey tea and you some coffee while you read the article. Did you miss me while I was gone?"

"I got so busy, I forgot you were gone. I tried to call a few times. No answer. There you were, having the time of your life, Ms. Activist."

Marge was full of questions after she finished the article. "I can't wait to hear your side of the story," Marge said.

Ethel told Marge what really happened, not what was reported in the newspaper.

“How's Cap't Rolly? How are you?” Marge's eyes were wide with shock.

Ethel said reassuringly, “Cap't Rolly has recovered from his beating. I'm in good health, thanks to Cap't Rolly's quick work.”

After dinner and the children put to bed, they sat back down at the kitchen table. They each had a renewed mug of coffee.

They sipped and looked at each other.

“Do you want to tell me something? I can see it in your eyes. Are you worried about how I might take it?” Marge asked.

“You sure can read me. Please listen, no questions until I finish, okay?” Ethel said as she took hold of Marge's hands.

She was linking the two of them like connecting computers. She wanted them to be on the same mental page.

Ethel closed her eyes. "When I was in a coma, I almost died. I had a near-death experience. I saw Steve. We met, we walked together. He didn't talk. He used signs to show me. I saw his smiling face. He's happy."

Marge pulled her hands away from Ethel's. One hand went to her mouth.

She whispered, “Oh my.”

“I've not told this experience to anyone but you. We need the answer to why Steve died and who killed him. He did not kill himself and it was not an accident." Ethel stopped and took a breath. "Someone murdered him."

She reached out an took Marge's hands again. "Do you believe me, Marge?"

She reacted automatically. She pulled her hands away and pulled inside herself, like a threatened snail.

Marge nodded. "I believe you. I never thought about someone killing Steve. This concept of murder is new."

Ethel saw that the word murder hit Marge like a blow.

"No one is after us. If they are, they've waited a long time." Ethel paused. "Per my vision, I think it's someone from Alberta."

Marge sat quietly for a long time.

Ethel sat, thinking that Marge needed time to digest those words.

"I wonder what happened in Alberta? Steve mentioned no real problems. He didn't much like his cousin or his living circumstances, but no problems or bad issues." Marge speculated out loud. "I accepted his death as a mystery."

Ethel frowned and said, "I can't let it go. I need to know why. Do you think we can figure it out?"

Marge furrowed her brow. "I solve mathematical problems for half the business' in Sechelt. I'm a problem solver. But this...how will we do this?"

Ethel noticed a subtle change in their conversation. The word 'we' had crept in.

Their coffee got cold as they talked. Ethel stood and poured enough in, warming up their mugs. They sat silently stirring their coffee.

Ethel's work at the Lodge meant she often faced mysterious deaths, which she solved with copious records and autopsies. Mysteries did not stay mysterious for long. She had lots of facts. In this case, all she had was her near-death experience to solve Steve's mysterious death.

As they sat, the clock ticked off another half hour.

Marge broke the silence. “We need a plan. Let's figure this out. Have you any ideas?”

Ethel did.

Together, they made a plan.

Ethel would arrange for the bus tickets and hotel in Alberta. Patti would take care of the children, water the plants, and feed Q. Marge would call the school to tell them to allow Patti to pick them up; she would call her clients to tell them she would be unavailable.

They planned to leave the day after tomorrow.

Chapter Thirteen

Ethel's day started when two children jumped on her bed and gave her big hugs. They woke her from her dream of Steve's smiling face.

She shooed them out of the room so she could get dressed. Then she went to the kitchen.

Marge stood at the stove, making coffee.

She said, “Good morning. How did you sleep last night?”

“Great! I saw Steve's smile in my dreams. How was yours?”

“Mine was better than a couple of days ago. I guess I'm almost used to Steve's forever absence.”

“I've never gotten totally used to Ian being gone.”

Marge handed her a cup of coffee. “I dream about Steve, too.”

“We need to find the facts about what happened.”

Marge nodded. “Can you drop the kids off at school? I need to catch up on my billings and bookkeeping so I can be ready to leave for Alberta.”

“Sure.”

“Thanks. I'll pick them up after school.”

“I need to get a few things done at the Lodge and tell the staff about going out of town for a few days.”

“Okay. I have a two o'clock appointment with Dr. Andy, the vet in Sechelt. Q needs her yearly check-up and shots.” Marge paused. “Do you remember Andy? He was on Steve's high school football team.”

“I remember him,” Ethel said. “I didn't know he was still around town.”

“After high school, he joined the Air Force and because a pilot. A few years later, he went back to school to become a veterinarian. Now he's a member of the CFVC”

“What is CFVC?”

“Canadian Flying Vet Corps. They bring supplies to rural provincial areas and the Northern Territories. He does surgeries remotely as needed.”

“I see.”

“The also move pets from overloaded animal shelters. On top of his flying vet services, he has a thriving business here on the coast.” She paused. “He wasn't at the funeral. Maybe he doesn't know Steve's dead. I'll tell him when I drop off Q.”

Ethel set her empty cup on the counter. “The kids are ready to leave. I am, as well. See you later. Call if you need anything from the market.”

She gave Marge a quick hug before she walked out the door.

“Come on, kids,” she called. “Get in the car. Let's go.”

The children scrambled into the car and off they went.

Whizzing down the highway, Ethel thought about the last email Steve had sent to her. He had written, 'Will has gotten progressively hostile. I've been sick. I cut out of work for two days in a row. Next week cannot come soon enough. I can't wait to leave. I'm so happy my six months are over. But Ken, the boss, offered me another job. I'll talk to you about it when I get home. Just in case I take the job, I'll leave some of my things here.'

Ethel dropped the children at the schoolyard with a kiss and a wave.

She drove to the Lodge, still thinking about Steve's email. She got an email every week from him. Most were fun and simple with a story about the mine. But not that last email.

The phone rang as she entered her office.

Cap't Rolly was on the line.

"I've some unsettling news about your narrow escape from death," he said. "We assumed the poison came from the taco stand."

"Yes. I know it did. That was the only food I ate that morning." She forgot all about the email.

"The Health Department investigated the taco stand and found nothing. As far as the authorities are concerned, the taco stand is clean."

"I got the poison there. I know I did." She paused. "I need to tell you. Marge and I leave tomorrow to go to Alberta. We will find the answer to why someone murdered Steve. And with the same poison that almost killed me."

"Be careful."

"We will. If the poison didn't come from the taco stand, then maybe the answer is in Alberta and the mine. It might have something to do with Will. According to Steve's emails, Will turned out to be a sleazeball. I will find the truth."

"Call me while you're there. Keep me in the loop."

"I will. Thanks for the update from the Health Department."

Ethel just finished telling the staff how to cover in her absence when Marge came in.

Her daughter-in-law grinned from ear to ear. She carried Q in a cat carrier.

"I've got a healthy cat. She's fine for another year."

"That's got you grinning like that?"

Marge shook her head, eyes twinkling. "Are you done here? We need to talk."

"Yes. I'm finished. What's up?"

"I have news."

"I'm listening."

"How would you like to fly to Alberta?"

"What?"

"I told Dr. Andy about Steve and what we needed to find out. He has a surgery and supplies to drop off tomorrow at a farm near where we need to go. He lands on the mine's airstrip." Without waiting for Ethel to respond, she said, "Do you want to fly to Alberta?"

Ethel saw the excitement all over Marge's face. She was as excited as a little child.

"A quick trip, no bus or ferry. I like that. When would we leave?"

"I'll drop the kids off at school and pick you up. Then we'll to go Sechelt's airport. By eleven o'clock, we'll land at the mine's airstrip. Dr. Andy has a pickup there with CFVC already. He can drop us off at the hotel."

"When does he fly back here?"

"The surgery and follow-up will take two days. We can investigate for the answer during those days. On Friday, we will return. Patti will pick the kids up from school tomorrow and keep them until we get back."

Ethel gave Marge a quick hug. "You have an excellent plan."

"We can bring two small boxes back with us. Dr. Andy says he will offload supplies and there will be room for Steve's stuff. What do you think?"

"Let's do it. I'll pack tonight. What time will you pick me up in the morning?"

"Right after I drop the kids at school. I'll be there by nine. We'll be at the mine before eleven to start our investigation."

"I told Cap't Rolly we were off to Alberta. But I didn't tell him how we would get there. I'll see you in the morning."

Ethel had flown commercial jets, but she had not been on a private plane before.

She was excited.

Ethel knew Marge was eager to fly. Sleepovers at Patti's would be fun for the children. Q would guard the mouse hole behind the stove.

Patti had confided in Ethel the week before. "I'm happy to help Marge in whatever way I can. Life has been hard for her these past six months. I often see tears when she comes over for coffee."

The next morning, Ethel was on her porch waiting with her suitcase when Marge pulled up to the house.

The Sechelt airport served private planes and a few

emergency aircraft, such as fire and rescue helicopters. The letters CFVC on the side of an airplane announced its use.

Two men checked the plane. Ethel assumed the man with the golden retriever by his side was Dr. Andy and the other man was a maintenance man or plane mechanic.

The preliminary check finished, the man with the dog waved the women over.

"Hi, I'm Dr. Andy," he said to Ethel.

She shook his hand. "I remember when you played football with Steve."

"A long time ago. I'm sorry for your loss."

"Thank you."

"We have another passenger today. His name is Frankie. He flies with me on my trips. His job is to calm down sick, scared, or wounded animals that need transporting. I don't know how he does it, but it works."

While he talked about Frankie, Ethel bent down and offered the dog her hand. "Hi Frankie, happy to meet you."

Frankie licked her hand.

Dr. Andy continued, "You're neither sick nor wounded, but Frankie will ride with us. I have to bring a cat back."

They walked to the plane.

"Put your bags behind your seats when you get in," he said. "Then buckle up. We can take off now. The weather's clear and the flight path looks smooth."

Marge and Ethel followed Andy's instructions.

The flight lasted an hour.

They landed smoothly.

The time zone changed as they flew east; they arrived an hour later than Ethel had expected.

Dr. Andy gave them a ride to the only hotel in town.

They thanked him and walked into the hotel to register.

After they put their suitcases in their room, Marge asked, "It's lunchtime here. What do you want to do?"

"Let's eat now. I can call Will after the shift changes or catch him walking home. I didn't tell him we planned to come. It's our chance to see his house and Steve's room as he left it."

They found a cafe conveniently located next door to the hotel.

A siren blew to let the miners, and the entire town, know it was lunch break.

Marge said, "Let's sit at that table by the window."

They ordered their lunch and watched the miners troop in. Most of the men went to the washroom. One guy went directly to the counter and sat on a stool by himself.

"That's Will," said Ethel. "I'd recognize his face anywhere. He looks just like his worthless father, my ex-brother-in-law."

She watched him as the waitress served their lunch.

Ethel whispered to Marge, "What do you think? Should I go over and scare him off the stool? Or should I phone him first?"

Marge picked up her sandwich, took a bite, and chewed thoughtfully before swallowing and answering. "Scare him!" She took another bite.

With a twinkle in her eye, Ethel said, "Watch this."

She walked over and sat on the stool next to Will.

"Hi Will. I'm your Aunt Ethel. Do you remember me?"

Will startled and nearly fell off his stool. He had to hold on to it to keep his balance.

"W-w-when did you get here? I didn't know you planned to come here. Where's Steve? Did he come back with you?"

"Why do you ask that?"

"'Cuz he left gear here. I thought he'd be back."

"No. He's not coming back. We're here to pick up his things from your house. Tell me the address and we'll walk over."

"I get off at three. I'll stop at the hotel and pick you up. You can walk with me. It's not far."

"We'll meet you here at three," Ethel said. "I'll let you get back to your lunch, and I'll do the same."

The smirk on a few miners' faces as she returned to the table told her they did not like Will.

Ethel finished eating her lunch.

Marge sipped her coffee, busy talking about their plan.

A tall man walked up to their table. His shadow fell across Ethel's plate.

She looked up and asked, "May we help you?"

The man said, "No, but maybe I can help you."

"How?" she asked. "We don't know you. How do you know who we are?"

"My name is Kenneth Hastings. People call me Ken. I'm the Personnel Manager at the mine. I hired Steve."

"You knew Steve?" Marge asked. "Would you like to sit and join us?"

"Thanks." He pulled out a chair and sat down. "No one comes or goes in this small town without us knowing about it. When

Andy's plane landed, I saw you two get off."

"We're here to pick up the things Steve left behind," Marge said quietly.

"He isn't coming back for the job I offered him?"

"No," said Ethel. She saw the tears in Marge's eyes. "I'm sorry. Steve cannot take your job offer."

Wanting to keep Ken's focus away from the teary-eyed Marge, she continued, "What did Steve to on the job? He didn't talk about it."

Knowing about Steve's work and his relationships with his co-workers and supervisors was essential to their investigation.

They talked for a couple of hours. Ken answered all their questions.

Except for the most important question. Why would anyone want to kill Steve?

The women could not ask Ken that question. They had to discover the answer themselves.

The mine siren blew, announcing the end of the day shift. Will would walk by at any moment.

Ethel got up and paid their bill. She thanked Ken for telling them so much about the mine and Steve's job.

Ken's parting words were, "I'm sorry Steve won't return. He was a real asset to the mine. I wanted to promote him to shift boss. He'll always have a job here."

As he said those words, Will walked by the window.

Ethel and Marge hurried to meet him.

Chapter Fourteen

The women met Will on the sidewalk.

Ethel said, “Will, I want to introduce you to Marge. Steve's wife. We wanted to thank you for letting Steve rent a room from you.”

Will glanced at Marge. “Glad to meet you,” he mumbled. “I was happy I could do this favor for Aunt Ethel.”

It was a short walk to Will's house. Passing through the gate, a path led through the unkempt yard full of junk and weeds to the front door.

“Come in,” Will said. “I plan to watch the hockey match this afternoon. I just came home to change clothes.”

As they stood in the entry, Ethel saw stacks of empty, dusty old beer cans and food containers. She realized Will's sole concern was eating, drinking, and the job. What she saw confirmed Steve's emails.

She had shared the last email from Steve with Marge. He had written, 'I've discovered the truth about this lying rat. He's lived rent-free while I paid the full price. I'm concerned about his lying and cheating. He's up to something. I wonder what it is. I cannot wait to get out of here and back home.'

Will cleared the junk and garbage off the couch. “Have a seat.” He sat on an old recliner in front of the television.

Ethel said, “We won't stay long. We're here to see what Steve left. Then, we'll get boxes to pack up his things. We need to see what he left so we know how many boxes to get.”

“Okay. I'll be gone. But I'll leave the house unlocked for you.”

“Okay. Thanks. I'd like to take you to dinner tonight. My treat. Where can I meet you?”

“I'll be at the pub watching the game. It's over about five-thirty. It has great ribs. And it's across the street from the hotel. How about meeting there? I'll get us a table.”

“It's a date. See you there at five-thirty.” She grinned at him. “By the way, can you give me the FedEx and post office schedules and your work schedule?”

“Sure.” Will picked up a piece of paper from the floor and wrote on it. “Here's my work schedule. The FedEx is open from nine-to-nine. And the post office is open from nine-to-five.”

“Thanks.” She took the paper from him and stuffed it into her purse. “Going to dinner with you will be fun. It's been a long time since we got together.”

“Yeah.”

Will did not look as though he thought spending an evening with his old aunt would be fun.

“We'll be back as soon as we get boxes. Where's Steve's room?”

Will pointed to a doorway. “That one. Make yourself at home. I gotta get ready to go to the pub.” He got up and walked into another room.

Ethel got up, held her breath, and entered Steve's room. She had to see how he lived in this polluted house.

His room was clean, neat, and orderly.

She saw what she needed to see and closed the door. She looked at Marge.

Marge had not gotten off the couch.

She said, “I cannot look and touch the leftovers of his life yet. Too many memories to face.”

“That's okay. I know what we need.”

They left the house after thanking Will for his time and opening his house to them.

Ethel knew boxing up Steve's life would challenge for both of them. *I've done it before, and I can do it again,* Ethel thought sadly.

Walking beside Ethel, Marge said, “I hate this. But we must do it.”

“I could tell how you felt. You wanted to wring Will's neck. I wanted to, as well. We'll search for any evidence of poison, pack up Steve's things, find the truth, and leave as quickly as possible.”

They passed the hotel and continued down the street to the FedEx office in the market.

“I think two boxes are enough,” Ethel said. “Let's buy two medium-sized and get back while Will is out of the house.”

Ethel thought the second visit to the house would be no more manageable than the first. She asked, “Are you ready to go back?”

Marge was unable to say yes. Instead, she nodded and said, “I'll try.”

After they bought the boxes, they returned to Will's house and knocked on the door.

No one answered.

There was a note on the counter inside. 'Left to watch hockey at the pub. See you later.'

Said Ethel, “I'll go into his room and pack. You check everywhere in the house for poison.”

Ethel packed. She left the mining equipment, but took the sheets, towels, sleeping bag, books, and paperwork. She finished filling the boxes and carried them to the front gate.

Marge followed her outside.

“I did a thorough job searching the entire house, every room, even Will's closet,” Marge said. “My investigation found filthy, stinky, dirty places everywhere and an ancient, rusty tin of rat poison under the kitchen sink. That's all. Where else could he hide it?”

“I don't know unless he keeps it at the mine. We may have to ask Ken if we can get into Will's locker there.”

“As I searched, I looked out the window and saw a shed in the backyard. Let's go look in it.”

They found their way through the weeds to the shed.

Undisturbed, empty bottles covered in cobwebs, and dust sat on a table. The sun lit a row of small bottles on a ledge above the window.

“Look! Someone handled one of the bottles on that sill,” Ethel said. “It shines with no dust.”

“You're right!”

“But we brought nothing to get a sample with. Some sleuths

we are."

"I'll get a sample of it when you take Will for dinner."

"Are you sure you can come back here alone?"

"Yes."

Ethel glanced at Marge and saw the stubborn thrust of her chin. She knew that look. She had seen it often enough in the turbulent years of their relationship.

"I want to find out who killed my husband. Don't worry about me."

They retraced their steps back to the street.

Ethel saw Ken driving down the street. She waved at him to stop.

When he rolled down his window, she asked, "Is there a taxi in town? We need help to get these boxes to the airstrip."

He laughed. "No taxis. But I'm here. Let's put them in my pickup and I'll take them to the plane for you."

"Thanks. They're too heavy for us to carry very far."

"Let me load them for you" He opened his door. "I'll take you to the airstrip. Andy and I are supposed to meet when he finishes his surgery this afternoon. Come on. Ride with me. We'll check to see if Andy has returned. Then I'll give you a ride to the hotel."

Ethel agreed and got in the pickup

She saw Marge hesitate.

"I want to take a bath," Marge said. "Will's place is filthy. I want to wash Will right out of my life. He's a slimy jerk."

Ken made a face in agreement.

"I'll walk to the hotel. I need fresh air. You don't need me at the airstrip. You have two muscular guys with Ken and Dr. Andy to load the boxes." She turned away from the pickup and walked toward the hotel.

As he drove, Ken radioed their plan to Andy.

Andy and Frankie waited by the plane when Ken drove up.

The men put the boxes on the plane.

Andy put Frankie in the pickup's bed and hopped in beside Ethel.

"Hi," said Ethel. "Thanks for lifting the boxes."

"No problem," Dr. Andy said. "Where's Marge? Is she okay?"

"She walked to the hotel. She felt grimy after being in Will's house and wanted to bathe."

"I wanted to ask if one of you two could take Frankie for a walk? He needs to stretch his legs. I've kept him in all day. I've business to talk over with Ken. We'll be in the hotel bar."

"I'll ask Marge when I get to our room. I think we can walk Frankie now that we've packed up Steve's stuff."

Ken parked the pickup, and they all walked into the hotel.

When she got to their room, Ethel told Marge Andy's request.

"I think it's a perfect guise for wandering around town," she said as she finished the tale.

"I agree," said Marge. "I'll take Frankie back to Will's with me."

"Great. Now I must get ready for my date. Yuk!"

"We haven't compared notes since leaving Will's house," Marge said.

"You're right. Tell me what all you saw."

"I told you about the rat poisoning under the sink. We both saw the clean bottle in the shed. We need to send samples to Cap't

Rolly. I don't want Will to suspect us. We must be careful not to disturb anything."

"Be sure to toss out the gloves after you get the samples. We need to protect ourselves. You know how lethal that poison is, even on skill or breathed in from the air."

"I'll buy baggies and surgical gloves before I go. There is a pharmacy down the street. I'll take my cell phone for photos. Rat poison is a banned substance in Canada, but you never know. I'll get a sample from each container."

"I agree with your plan. Do you think an hour is long enough? I don't think I can stand Will for more than an hour."

"Yes."

"Remember, inhale nothing. Buy a face mask, too."

"If you think I want to inhale anything in that scumbag's house, you're wrong."

I'm meeting Will at five-thirty. You'll have an hour to take Frankie for his detective walk."

"That should do. It's not far. While you're at dinner, Frankie and I will collect the samples. Don't worry about it. FedEx stays open late. If we send it tonight, we can get an answer back early tomorrow."

"Marge, I'm a good general, but you're better at planning."

Marge grinned and agreed.

At five-thirty, Ethel and Marge walked downstairs.

Marge walked into the hotel bar where the men sat with Frankie.

Ethel walked across the street to a country-western pub.

Will waved to her from a booth with a red-checkered

tablecloth.

She slid into the seat across from him.

The jukebox music blared, making it near impossible to visit.

Ethel wanted to get him talking while they waited for their bar order.

Will fidgeted and drummed his fingers nervously.

The waitress came for their drink orders.

Ethel asked for a cola.

Will ordered a shot of whiskey with a beer chaser.

When the waitress brought their drinks, they ordered their dinners.

While they waited for their food, Ethel asked Will unimportant family questions.

Ethel nursed her cola through three of Will's refills. The liquor worked on Will's inhibitions.

When their dinner arrived, she figured it was time to ask her pre-planned questions.

“Steve's hard to get along with at home. How was he here? Did he cause you any trouble?”

Will was eager to tell her everything he made up. “Steve did as little as possible. The crew thought the same. I kept him on because he paid half the rent.”

With more snide remarks, Ethel realized Will was jealous of Steve's leadership ability.

She remembered Ken's opinion and comments. They were the opposite of Will's views.

Ethel checked her watch, hoping she could leave the noisy pub soon. She could not stand Will's grandiose opinion of himself.

She saw right through his lies.

After the meal, Ethel faked indigestion. "My stomach's upset. You know if is easy to get sick in a strange place. I'll get the tab. You stay and enjoy yourself."

She paid the bill and returned to the table with another round for Will.

"My evening was great," he said. "Thanks for dinner. You're an old sweetie."

Will stood as if to walk her out, but he went to the bar with his drinks in hand instead.

Ethel watched. No one offered to talk to him or buy him a beer. That told her a lot about Will's friends. He had none.

She hurried to her room at the hotel.

Marge anxiously waited for her. She showed her mother-in-law an envelope containing two baggies. One had a cotton ball, and the other had the rat poison sample. She had written a note as well.

"Cap't Rolly called while you were out and said to send the samples to the medical examiner's office. He'll call us with the results tomorrow."

"We should hurry to the FedEx office before it closes. If you're ready, let's go."

The women hurried to the FedEx office a few blocks away.

After posting their small package to be sent that night, they returned to their room to discuss their notes.

Getting to Alberta was Part One of their plan. Done.

Part Two was to find evidence against Will based on what Steve had written in his emails. Done.

They had just finished Part Three, overnighting the evidence to Cap't Rolly.

Ethel stared into space. Her mind was full of questions. *How do we prove Steve's death was murder? What had they discovered in Will's house? I know we'll have answers in the morning.* Out loud, she said, "We can't let his murder go unnoticed!"

"I'm worried that the local RCMP might not believe us," Marge said. "We're not real police detectives."

Ethel nodded. "They didn't believe me when I told them in Vancouver that it was the tacos that poisoned me. They didn't even believe Cap't Rolly about the dead fish."

They both said, "How do we get the RCMP to believe us?" They grinned at each other.

"We need a new plan." They said at the same time and laughed.

With Marge's analytical logic and Ethel's persistence, they constructed a new strategy.

Ethel called Cap't Rolly and laid it all out

He agreed.

"Our heads are reeling from today's activities," Ethel said. "How about a movie to slow us down?"

"Sure. I'll check."

Moments later, Marge said, "There's only one movie channel. And the only thing about to start is a werewolf movie. Are you into that?"

"No, but sure, why not?"

They laughed, put on their pajamas, and got ready for the scary movie.

Chapter Fifteen

The phone ringing persistently woke Ethel up to level one – almost awake. She answered with her eyes half-closed and her voice sleepy. The more she listened, the straighter she sat up and the wider her eyes opened.

Hanging up the phone, she quickly threw on her sweatsuit and rushed out to find Marge.

Ethel found her daughter-in-law enjoying a peaceful cup of coffee in the cafe.

"Cap't Rolly just called," she said breathlessly. "He got our sample. It is poison. It is the poison."

"Yes! We did it. Now what?"

"He's set things in motion at the medical examiner's office in Vancouver, implementing our plan. They called the Superintendent of the entire Alberta RCMP rather than just the local office here in this town." She paused. "Marge, they believed us."

Marge gulped. "Wow. They liked our plan and detective work. They believed our words. I can't tell you how relieved and excited I feel right now. What else did Cap't Rolly say?"

"The RCMP Superintendent listened to both Dr. Lowe and

Cap't Rolly give the results of the sample. The Superintendent said everything points to Will as the murderer. He said we should wait for the local RCMP to contact us."

"Are we ready if the RCMP calls us to come to the station?"

"Not me," Ethel retorted. "I need coffee and to get properly dressed. I cannot meet the Sargent like this. I haven't even brushed my teeth or combed my hair!"

Marge laughed. "I'll finish my coffee and bring you a cup."

The call had rattled Ethel. She hated upsetting her routine or plans. She went to dress, knowing Marge would soon bring her the needed coffee.

Shortly, Marge entered their hotel room.

"Here's your coffee. I had just finished mine when Dr. Andy walked in. He joined me and ordered coffee to go. Frankie wasn't with him."

"Thanks for the coffee. I bet Frankie isn't allowed in the cafe."

"Dr. Andy told me he has surgery on a sick cat this morning. I said that we'd be happy to walk Frankie. And that the dog can stay with us in our room today."

"Okay. What's his room number? I'll go get him and bring him to our room."

"Room twenty-five. He said he'd leave the door unlocked for us."

Ethel gulped the coffee Marge gave her. "Thanks Marge. I feel more like myself already."

Ethel set the empty cup down and went to get Frankie.

She brought him and his leash to their hotel room.

"I guess we'd better wait for the call before we take Frankie for his morning walk."

But waiting was very difficult, or nearly impossible, for Ethel. She waited about ten minutes.

"I can't just sit here and wait." She paced the room. "I need to do something."

Frankie watched her, wagging his tail.

"Why don't you take him for a walk," Marge said.

"I think I will. Cap't Rolly told me another thing I can check out while walking the dog. He said the tailings from the mine blasting would have trillium residue. It might be enough to kill fish. If I see water, I'll get samples."

"Good idea. I'll stay and wait for the phone call. Take your cell phone so I can reach you when the RCMP calls."

"Okay. I'll walk to the mine entrance at the end of this street. Maybe I can talk to the head of security. He may add information about the runoff and also about Will. Frankie and I should be back in thirty minutes."

"I bought a crossword puzzle book at the market. I'll get sit here and do a puzzle while I wait for the call."

Ethel put on her jacket. She stuffed baggies and cotton balls into the pockets. Then, she and Frankie went out to gather more evidence.

The street ended at the entrance to the mine, and a guard shack. A sign read, 'Employees and Authorized Visitors Only.' The placard 'Security Office' hung over the shed's door.

It was not much of a building, but it would keep a guard protected in inclement weather.

A trickling stream flowed from the mine behind the shed and

down the hill toward the valley below.

A man sat in the shed, reading a book. He propped hi feet on the edge of an old pot-bellied stove.

Ethel smiled at him as she knocked on the door frame and entered the room.

“Is there a tour?” she asked. “I'm curious about this new way to mine. I'm Ethel and this is Frankie. We're out for his morning walk.”

“Hi. Come on in.” He took his feet down and stood, holding his hand out. “I'm Dennis, head of the mine security. Nice to meet you, Ethel. Frankie, I already know; he's Dr. Andy's dog.”

They shook hands and exchanged grins.

Blushing a bit, Dennis released her hand. “Ah, yeah. I mean, yes, I'll show you around. It's rare for Frankie to bring visitors. He likes to sit by my stove and nap.”

Dennis picked up a radio and called someone. “Hey. I'm on a visitor's mission. Come to the shack and monitor the box.”

An indistinct voice answered, “Yes, sir.”

“The Box is what we call the security office,” he said to Ethel. “That guard is out walking the mine perimeter. He'll be here soon.”

“Okay.” Ethel looked around as she tried to figure out how she would get a sample of the stream of water by the shed.

“The mine is an open-pit that covers many acres of land. We provide security for the circumference, as well as in the mine itself.”

“Does it need that much security?”

“Attempted illegal entry is common.”

The guard arrived.

Dennis nodded to him and took Ethel's elbow.

"Frankie can stay here and help guard the Box while I show you around."

Ethel kept up a conversation throughout the tour.

Dennis liked to talk and did not leave out any details.

As they crossed the small stream, she asked, "Does this water come from the mine proper?"

"All water from this area is runoff. We, er, I mean the mining company, filters all water flowing from the mine. Farmland downstream is safe from contaminants."

Ethel slipped a baggie out of her pocket and knelt by the water before Dennis could object.

"Dr. Andy asked me to nab a little sample for some study."

When she stood, Dennis had an odd look on his face.

"Thanks, Dennis," she said. "You conducted a fascinating tour. It was very interesting."

"No problem." He smiled again. "I rarely get to show a classy lady around. Please come back anytime. You're splendid company. It gets lonesome out here by myself."

"I wish I could stay longer and visit. Maybe I'll come back later." She winked at him before turning to walk away.

She had hardly gotten out of sight before her cell phone rang.

"They called," Marge said without preamble. "The RCMP wants to talk to us."

"Frankie and I'll be there as quickly as we can."

"I've already left the hotel. Meet you at the RCMP office."

Ethel entered the station and saw Marge sitting on a chair in a small office. Ethel joined her. Frankie lay at her feet, panting.

“Sitting here alone, before you came, was almost too difficult,” Marge whispered. “I cannot tell our story without crying.”

Ethel scooted her chair closer to Marge and took her daughter-in-law's hand.

“I feel that way, too. We loved the same man. I love you and the kids as much as I loved Steve. We're making things right for Steve. I'll do the talking, if you want.”

“Please.”

Ethel squeezed Marge's hand.

“We're a team. You're not alone.”

Ethel gave Marge a hug, which pulled Frankie, leash and all, into the hug. The women both giggled at the silly way Frankie joined their hug.

Ethel dropped the leash. Frankie moved to the far side of the room. No more hugging for him.

An officer entered. He put a file and a recorder on the desk.

Both women looked at him expectantly.

“Hello. I'm Officer Clancy. I'm heading this case.” He sat down after shaking their hands. “Tell me the entire story. I got statements from the Vancouver office and from the Chief Constable in Edmonton. I'll record your statement.”

He started the recording by identifying all those in the room, plus the day and time.

Ethel started at the beginning, with Steve losing his job. She included all the details. Maybe too many details.

Officer Clancy interrupted. “What's the point?”

She told about Steve's death. “And then someone poisoned me with the same poison that killed my son,” she said.

"How do you know?"

Marge spoke. "I gathered samples from Will's shed and sent them to be analyzed by the medical examiner in Vancouver."

When they finished, Officer Clancy hit the stop button and said, "That's quite a story. We need proof."

"I thought the samples I collected from Will's place was the proof."

"No. That's evidence."

"How will you prove it?"

"Leave that to us. That's our job"

He gathered his file and the recorder. He stood to leave.

"One more question," he said, looking at Marge. "Did you touch or move the bottle where you got the sample of the poison with your bare hands?"

"No. I wore surgical gloves, and I replaced the bottle exactly as I found it. I also took photos with my cell phone."

"Send them to me. I'll give you the number."

While they did that, Ethel retrieved Frankie and his leash.

"Done," Marge said. "I sent the photos."

"Go back to your hotel room and stay there," Officer Clancy said. "Don't speak to anyone about this. Especially do not speak to Will Drake."

"May we eat lunch?" Ethel asked.

Officer Clancy smiled. "Yes, go ahead and eat. But discuss nothing about why you're in Alberta. Too many ears, know what I mean?"

"Too late," said Ethel. "Everyone knows we came with Dr. Andy to get Steve's things. We've said nothing about his death or what killed him. Dr. Andy knows, but no one else. Will thinks Steve might come back, because we left all his mining gear."

"Okay. Just, it's better not to talk to anyone at this point, in case something slips."

He ushered the women and dog toward the door.

"We'll call you as soon as we have proof and Will confesses. We'll need you to identify the bottle of poison. Plan to come back to the office when we call."

Ethel glanced at the clock on the wall. It was already two-thirty. No wonder her stomach growled.

"You need to get out of here before shift changes and any miner sees you here, especially Will."

He guided them to the door.

As they left, Ethel overheard two officers talking.

"He has to walk right by here."

"We'll join him on his way home."

"Then we'll all arrive together."

"We'll have him show us his shed."

"Yeah, if he lets us in, we won't have to get a search warrant."

Ethel took Marge's arm as the women walked away.

Chapter Sixteen

The women hurried to the cafe.

Ethel said, “A light lunch is a good idea if your stomach is upset.”

“It's turning flips.”

“Order what you think will soothe our guts. I'll take Frankie to Dr. Andy's room. He should be okay in there alone. We want to be ready to leave quickly when they call.”

Marge arrived in their room with apple pie à la mode and milkshakes.

Ethel laughed. “Comfort food, for sure. Let's eat.”

They ate quietly.

“I wish I had my knitting,” said Ethel.

“I have my crossword puzzle book. Would that help?”

The siren blew. It was three o'clock. Time for shift change. Time for Will to get off work.

Ethel mindlessly watched television while Marge worked on a crossword.

“Are you as scared as I am?” Marge asked. She put her book down. “I hate waiting to find out if we were right.”

"Yes." Ethel paused. "I know what you mean." She spoke thoughtfully. "If Will can tell the truth. He's such a liar. But in my heart, I know he's responsible for Steve's death."

"I hope our evidence proves he did it and he cannot wiggle out of it. The poison was his. It was in his shed. We know that, don't we?"

"You found it in his shed. We both saw it. Of course, it is his."

"What will we do until they call? I can't concentrate on my puzzle."

"Not knowing what's going on makes my stomachache more."

"It's almost five-thirty. We've heard nothing yet."

Said Ethel, "It's too quiet."

She jumped when the phone rang.

Marge sat closer to the phone and answered it after the first ring.

Yet Ethel heard the conversation.

"This is Officer Clancy. Come to the station. We're ready for you now."

"Okay," Marge said. "We're on our way."

She hung up the phone and looked at her mother-in-law.

Taking a deep breath, she said, "This is it."

They hurried to the police station.

An officer, who did not introduce himself, put them in a small holding area beside the interrogation room. There were only two chairs in the room.

The officer asked if they wanted to hear the interrogation going on in the other room.

Ethel said, “Yes, I do.”

Marge nodded.

He pushed a button. A screen moved aside from the one-way mirror and the speakers sounded.

“Will, tell us. Why did you do it? Why did you kill Steve O'Rourke?”

“I didn't!” Will blubbered. “He was fine when I gave him a ride to the bus station. I didn't kill him.”

“Will, Will, Will. Don't lie to us. You had the poison that killed Steve in your shed. You killed him. Admit it.”

“Okay, okay, okay. I admit I made the poison. But I didn't kill Steve with it.”

“Alright. Good, good. You made the poison. You gave it to your roommate. You killed Steve.”

“No! I made it, yes. And...and...and I gave him a little to make him sick so he wouldn't come back to the mine. But I didn't kill him.”

“Why didn't you want him to come back to the mine?”

“He was gonna get the promotion to shift boss. That was my job. I earned it. I worked here longer. But Steve walked in like he owned the place. The boss was ready to give him the shift upgrade. It was mine! I earned it!”

“So, you killed him because of a promotion?”

“No! I didn't kill him. I made him sick. That's all I did. I swear!”

Ethel watched as Officer Clancy lifted Will to his feet by his shirt collar and maneuvered him toward the door.

The officer with them pushed the stop button.

“Would you like to hear what happened when we went to his

place?"

Both women nodded.

"We walked Will into the shed and asked him what was in the bottle. He said trillium right off."

"Really?" Marge asked. "He confessed right then?"

"Not quite," the officer said. "We asked what he did with trillium. He said he sold it."

"He made it? I didn't think my nephew was smart enough to be a chemist."

"It's easy to make the poison. Will told us that he cleaned up the residue after they blasted the rock. The residue on the blasting caps, added to water, is the poison."

"That makes me sick. But how did you get him to confess?"

"We showed him the report from your Captain Rolly, the biologist. At that point, he collapsed and spilled his guts."

"That's when he confessed?" asked Ethel.

"No. There, as here, Will claims he didn't kill Steve. He says he put it in Steve's cola to make him sick. It wasn't clear if Steve drank the cola. But there was intent for Steve to drink it. Intent to kill."

Ethel took a deep breath and let it out slowly. It was a huge relief to have found the killer.

"What happens now?'

"Tomorrow we'll transfer Will to Edmonton for further questioning, arraignment, and charges. He'll probably ask for a lawyer. There will be more steps before we get a conviction. But he will stay in jail."

"I'm so relieved and happy we found the evidence to catch

him," Ethel said.

The officer smiled. "We couldn't have done it without you. Thank you."

He shook their hands.

"You're free to go home now."

For the first time since over-hearing the interrogation, Ethel noticed Marge seemed as if in a trance. She took her daughter-in-law's arm and led her out of the police station.

Ethel felt relieved and ready to eat dinner. But Marge did not seem to feel the same.

They walked are in arm to the hotel bar.

Ethel sat Marge at a table, sat across from her, and looked at her closely.

Since entering the police station at five-thirty, Marge had said only a few words. She was pale and her breathing was shallow.

"Marge!" Ethel spoke sharply. "Take a deep breath!"

Marge shuddered, blinked, and took a deep breath. Then she focused on Ethel.

"Is it all over?"

"Yes. It's over. Our job is done. We can go home."

Something wet licked Ethel's ankle.

She jumped and looked down.

Frankie nudged her leg.

Reaching down to pet the dog, she looked around the bar.

Dr. Andy and Ken walked toward them.

"May we join you?" asked Ken. "Word has it that Will is in jail."

“Yes. Have a seat.” Ethel did not clarify if her 'yes' was for the men to join them or for the news about Will.

Dr. Andy leaned forward and whispered, “Is it over?”

“Yes.” Ethel exclaimed rather loudly. “We're ready to go home. Do you fly back to Sechelt tomorrow?”

He nodded. “I plan to leave around ten in the morning if that works for you.”

“We'll be ready and checked out of our room after breakfast.”

“Good.”

Ethel could see the questions in the men's eyes.

“I need a glass of wine,” she announced.

“Do you have something to celebrate?” Ken pried.

“I think we're happy we got the packing job done,” Ethel remembered Officer Clancy's admonition not to talk to anyone about the investigation. “What do you think, Marge?”

Marge sat with her hands folded in her lap, staring off into space, unaware of her surroundings, until she heard her name.

“Did you say something? I'm sorry. I had my head in the clouds. I think I'll eat dinner and go straight to bed. This high mountain air is not like at the coast. I feel discombobulated.” She smiled vaguely at their table companions.

“Ethel,” she said. “You held me up, and I mean that literally. I couldn't have made it today without you. Thanks.”

With that, Marge stood and silently walked out of the bar without ordering her dinner.

Ethel ordered, ate, drank, and visited with Dr. Andy and Ken. They talked about many topics, but not about Steve or Will, death or murder.

Chapter Seventeen

Ethel felt mixed emotions when she boarded the plane for the trip home. Glancing at Marge's down-turned face, she saw a similar conflict.

She was happy they had solved the murder. But Ethel knew there would be a trial. She would have to relive and retell the story of Steve's death again.

Marge said, “I feel both happy and sad to go home. I really don't want to face the lonely house without Steve.”

Ethel patted her daughter-in-law's arm. “I understand. My house still feels empty without Ian.”

Dr. Andy loaded a sick cat in a cat carrier onto the plane.

They were airborne by ten-thirty.

The worried cat in the carrier gave Ethel a headache with her yowling. Frankie lay beside the carrier; his nose to the cage and the cat quit her screeching. His job, of calming sick or scared animals, worked. The rest of the flight was peaceful.

The one-hour trip climbing over the mountains to land in Sechelt took an hour, but because of the time zone change, they landed fifteen minutes after they took off.

As Marge disembarked, she said, “Thanks, Andy, for the trip. You made our detective work much easier.”

“You're welcome. I'm glad I could help.”

“I have a quick question for you,” Ethel said. “Did the town's people figure out Steve died?”

“They asked. Yesterday, after the RCMP arrested Will, I spilled the beans. I told Ken the reason you went to get Steve's things. The people working at the mine don't like Will.”

“We cannot thank you enough for the ride to and from Alberta.” She wanted to add that it had saved them a long bus ride and two ferry trips. Instead, she said, “I wonder if the Lodge needs a pet like Frankie. He's so loving and calm.”

Dr. Andy raised his eyebrows. “I'll keep my eyes open for a dog like Frankie. Many older folks have to give up their pets when they move into a nursing home.”

Marge said, “I'll go get the car from the parking area and come pick up you, our things, and Steve's boxes.”

“Okay.” Turning to Dr. Andy, Ethel said, “The responsibility of a resident pet is something I'll need to figure out.”

Once the women loaded their things, they waved goodbye to Dr. Andy.

When Marge pulled up to Ethel's house, Ethel asked, “Would you like to stay for a cup of coffee? You can stay until the kids get out of school. Or I can pick them up and bring them home.”

“I'll take a raincheck on the coffee,” Marge said. “I'm eager to get home and relieve Patty from her responsibilities at my house. Patti isn't used to taking care of the kids like you. They can ride the school bus home again. That's what Patti had them do.” She paused. “You've been my right-hand gal ever since Steve left seven months ago. I cannot get along without you. We've become a team.”

“I feel that way, too. We've discovered the best in each other. I don't want to run your life. I want to help you.”

“Don't get cocky on me,” Marge said in a sassy, laughing voice. “I have ideas about how I want to live my life. That's why I moved away from my parents. But you've worked with me, and I appreciate it. Thank you, Ethel, for being there for me.”

“I couldn't do anything else,” she said as she got out of the car. Before she shut the door, she said, “We have to focus on the kids. See you soon.”

Marge nodded her head as she drove away.

Ethel carried her suitcase toward the house. She planned to unpack, call Cap't Rolly, and then to go to the Lodge.

But when she got to her front door, there was a note from the nurse in charge of the Lodge.

The note worried Ethel. In her opinion, her staff could handle anything. She trusted their judgment. Dropping her suitcase inside the house, she hurried to the Lodge.

The nurse waited for Ethel in her office.

“I've never had to deal with a death at the Lodge since I started working here,” she said as she handed Ethel a clipboard with papers. “You always do the paperwork. I handled it the best I could. I hope I did it correctly. Please look it over carefully before signing off on it.”

“Let me look.”

Ethel said at her desk and flipped through the pages.

"Tell me what happened."

"The lady had a heart attack last night and passed around midnight. I called the doctor. He came and pronounced her dead. The coroner came for the body. This morning, I called her next-of-kin. I need to know if I forgot anything."

"It doesn't look as if you missed anything. Her room needs clearing. That's your next job. When is her family coming to get her personal effects?"

"I think they should be here any minute. They said they'd come here as soon as they made arrangements at the funeral home. I'll take care of the room right away. I was anxious to file all the papers properly."

"I'll file them now. Your paperwork is excellent. Good job."

The nurse smiled and left Ethel alone with her thoughts. *It's easy to deal with a resident's death, but not in your own family.*

She went to the filing cabinet. And hated the disorder.

Pulling out the entire stack of death files, she organized them in chronological order.

One file stood out.

Ethel remembered the odd death. It happened about seven months ago. She set the file aside to read through again.

She read the medical examiner's report. There were some anomalies with this lady's death, such as a blue tint to the skin and hair falling out. These signs had not bothered Ethel before. But now. It matched Steve's autopsy report.

Ethel quickly put all the files in the drawer except that one. She called Cap't Rolly.

"Hi," he said when he answered the phone. "I'm sailing to

Secret Cove today. I'll be back at my cabin tonight. How was your trip? I hear you got your nephew to confess to the poison."

"Yes, he confessed to making the poison and putting it in Steve's cola, but nothing more. He says he didn't kill Steve." She paused. "And I may believe him."

"What? What do you mean?"

"I'm concerned about a few facts. Specifically, timing."

"Explain."

"How long did the poison take to enter my bloodstream? It was less than an hour from the time I ate the taco until you saved my life, correct?"

"Yes. Maybe right at an hour."

"If Will poisoned Steve in Alberta, why did it take over fifteen hours for him to die in Sechelt? The timing is wrong."

"You're right! The timing doesn't add up!"

They both were silent on the phone.

Cap't Rolly continued, "I have some news about the fish. I did an extensive investigation of the water. It's not contaminated with trillium. Yet, dead and poisoned fish sill show up in the water by the ferry."

"Could the same person who poisons the fish be the same person who poisoned me and killed Steve?"

"I think so. But who? And why?"

"What else can you tell me about the poison?"

"Anyone who tastes it, touches it, or even smells it is in danger of brain damage or death."

"It's so powerful, I just cannot see where Will killed Steve. He must have had an accomplice."

Again, silence waxed over the phone.

Then Ethel said, “I almost forgot why I called. I discovered a report from the medical examiner's office on an autopsy of one of my residents who died seven months ago. The report mentions that her hair fell out after death and that her body was uniquely blue. But the M.E. called it an accidental death. No red flags as far as I can see. But what do you think? It sounds like Steve's autopsy report.”

“There could be a correlation between the two deaths. Give me the name, date, and details. I'll call Dr. Lowe.”

“Okay.” She rattled off the information.

“Got it.”

“This may help us find who. We know where and how. But the why is still a huge mystery.”

“We'll find out who, too.”

“What I wonder is, if it wasn't the taco, what made me sick? How did I ingest the poison?”

“Let me go to work with Dr. Lowe and the record department. With your information and the analysis of the poison sample from Alberta, we will discover your culprit. I think your nephew Will is still the key.”

“We're still missing a vital piece of the puzzle. I just don't know what it is.”

“We need proof and a confession. Will you be at Marge's house tonight? I'll come up after the kids go to bed with whatever I learn from Dr. Lowe.”

“Okay.” She sighed. “I'll wait for your results. Will you anchor in the Cove?”

“Yes, if it is open.”

“Okay. I'll see you tonight.

“Ethel, don't hang up! Do you have time to go to the RCMP's office in Sechelt for me? Inform them about how the road crew treated me. I may need protection or at least an increase of patrol near the cabin. The road crew made it very plain that they want me to leave the area.”

“Sure, I can do that.”

“I'll go to the RCMP office tomorrow and fill in the details. But I want them to know about the threats today.”

“No problem. Before I go to Marge's, I'll stop by their office. I'll write myself a note now so I don't forget.”

“The road crew have not completed the job on the highway yet. I think I'll be safer in Secret Cove than in Vancouver. Thanks for helping me out”

“You're welcome. See you at Marge's tonight.”

Ethel hung up and finished her filing.

The afternoon sped by quickly as she had much catching up to do at work.

Instead of going home to unpack, she headed to Marge's as soon as she closed her office for the night.

She stopped at the RCMP office and told the desk officer what Cap't Rolly told her.

The man wrote it down and promised they would be vigilant.

The sergeant came out of his office.

“I heard you talking. I recognized your voice.”

“Hello, Sergeant.”

“Wait a minute. I've received a summary report from the

Alberta office. Will Drake cooperated. He gave up the names of everyone to whom he'd sold trillium. He mentioned a cousin in Vancouver."

"A cousin? Steve was his only cousin here on our side of the family." *Hmm,* she thought. *Is there a cousin from his father's side of the family? I don't know those people.*

"He was adamant that he did not kill Steve. The investigation is back in our hands, on this end."

"I may have a clue for you to look into."

"Do tell."

"But I don't know for sure until tomorrow. Cap't Rolly will get a medical examiner's report on the trillium poisonings that happened on the North Shore over the past two years. If any names pop out, we may have our lead."

"We may, but you won't. Lead the sleuthing to us. Give us whatever information you find. And let us do our job."

"Aye, aye..."

Ethel left the office and drove to Marge's house and her grandchildren.

They met her at the door; welcoming her with hugs and kisses.

I never get welcomed like this at my house, she thought.

The children ran off to play.

Marge asked, "Coffee or something else to drink?"

"Coffee, please."

"I have things to tell you. You look as if you have something to tell me, too."

Ethel took the mug of coffee Marge handed to her and took a

sip. “You first.”

“Cap't Rolly is here. He's back until the weather is good for sailing. He came in tonight and anchored in his usual place. The kids spotted him and ran down to the pier to invite him to dinner tonight. He'll come up as soon as he gets settled into his cabin.”

“Great. We can find out what he discovered today. I called him. He told me the water was clean, but dead fish still show up in the bay.” She sighed. “I'm so happy to be back here with you and the children.”

“It's good to be back in my kitchen with my family.”

Ethel could tell that Marge wanted life to be normal more than anything else. No more murder investigations.

“Now my news,” Ethel said. “The RCMP in Alberta called our local office with the results of Will's interrogation. He is involved. He made the poison. And he gave Steven enough of it to make him sick. But a lethal dose is fast-acting.”

“What does that mean?”

“Will did not kill Steve. Someone on the pier or on the ferry did. We know it all started in Alberta. But murder happened in the Vancouver area.”

“You're doing a great job coordinating with the RCMP. I'm glad I can focus on mundane things like dinner and laundry.”

Cap't Rolly knocked at the door.

Marge hollered at the children to wash and get ready to eat.

The meal was delicious. Marge outdid herself.

Afterward, Ethel put the children to bed with extra kisses.

“I missed you guys,” she said. “I'm glad to be back with the two best children in the world.”

“We missed you, too,” Bobby said with a yawn.

“I'm glad you're back,” said Jennifer.

Ethel put Q on Bobby's bed and closed the door.

Marge topped off their coffee cups.

The women sat, waiting for Cap't Rolly's report.

He placed his cup on the table.

“I'm glad to be safe here in Secret Cove, again,” he said as he pulled a sheet of paper from his pocket and unfolded it.

“Dr. Lowe's inconclusive results put this investigation back in our hands.”

Said Ethel, “The RCMP told me that it was in their hands.”

He raised his eyebrows at her. “We know one of Ethel's resident's autopsy results was similar to Steve's.”

“No one claimed her body. There was no 'next-of-kin' listed in her file. All I know is she lived in the North Shore area.”

“May I look at her file? There may be a clue in it you missed.”

“Sure. I don't think that will violate any privacy contingency. Come to my office tomorrow. I'll give you the file to look through. Did you learn anything else today?”

“The trail ends with the Health Department placing a suspect in this vicinity.”

“So, we're still fishing for clues?” Ethel scratched her chin.

Marge smiled blankly at no one.

Cap't Rolly yawned. “I'll call it a night. I'll see you both tomorrow.”

He stood to let himself out and leave the two women sitting peacefully at the table.

Ethel called out to him softly. “Sleep comfortably. Good

night."

He shut the door behind himself.

The women sat in comfortable silence.

Ethel thought about what Cap't Rolly told them.

Marge looked at Ethel. "Would you like to come and live with us?"

The phone rang before they could say anything further.

Marge got up and hurried to answer it. She returned with a strange look on her face.

"I didn't want the phone ringing to wake the kids."

"Who was it?"

"An RCMP officer. He wants me to drive you to their office tomorrow."

"What for?"

"He said it was to identify someone."

"I can drive myself. What time do I need to be there?"

"Ten o'clock. But he insisted I drive you."

"I don't know why they need both of us, but okay."

"I'll call Patti in the morning and see if she can come over and watch the kids. They won't know she's here. They get so engrossed in Saturday morning cartoons."

Marge's earlier question dangled in the air.

Ethel was okay with not discussing it further. She needed time to decide to sell her house and move in with Marge. *Really, it's a dream come true.* The idea of living with Steve and his family had long been a fantasy. This was reality.

She would sleep on it and decide later.

Chapter Eighteen

It was nine-thirty on Saturday morning when Patti arrived in Marge's kitchen.

“Hi, Patti!” said Marge. “Thanks for watching the kids. We should be home before lunch.”

“It's fine. See you later.” Patti poured herself a cup of coffee.

Ethel waved a greeting to Patti as she and Marge gathered their purses and went out the door.

Marge got into the driver's side.

Ethel sat quietly in the passenger's seat.

“I can do without our habit of going to police stations,” Marge said.

Ethel nodded in agreement but said nothing during the drive. Something about this trip did not sit right with her.

As they entered the Sechelt RCMP office, Ether said to the officer sitting there, “We're here.”

The officer smiled at the women. “How can I help you today?”

“You seem surprised to see us,” said Ethel. “You knew we would be here.”

She glanced at Marge. Her daughter-in-law had a curious look on her face.

Ethel continued, "Your officer called us last night. He told Marge to bring me here at ten o'clock."

"I'll check the phone log." He looked at a notebook-like file on the counter. He shook his head. "I'm sorry, Ethel. There were no calls last night to Marge's house. We keep a record of all calls."

Marge angrily said, "Someone called us last night and told me to bring Ethel."

"No ma'am. I'm sorry, but no one called you from here. We logged your visit, Ethel, when you stopped by. I'm sorry you drove down here. We didn't call you."

"Something's wrong." Ethel immediately felt alarm bells in her brain. "Someone wanted us out of the house! Let's get to back to the house!" She glared at the officer. "Call for backup! Now!"

She turned and ran out of the office.

"Call Patti!" she yelled at Marge. "Tell her to lock the doors and don't let anyone in!"

Marge frantically dialed her phone as she ran to the car.

"The line is busy!" She got in the passenger's side. "I'll try again!"

Ethel slid into the driver's seat and dialed Cap't Rolly's number. Her stomach turned over. The construction guys might try to hurt or kidnap Patti and the children.

As Cap't Rolly answered, she immediately ordered him. "Get to the house. Now! Something's wrong. We're on our way with police backup."

She tossed the phone over her shoulder and started the

engine.

“Now the phone is dead!” wailed Marge.

Ethel gunned the motor and squealed the tires as she tore out of the parking lot.

She heard Marge quietly praying.

It took them almost twenty minutes at speeds just short of flipping the car to get home.

Ethel pulled into Marge's driveway. The RCMP pulled in the driveway as well.

Marge did not wait for Ethel to turn off the car. She jumped out, sprinted up the steps, and opened the door.

Ethel was right behind her.

They gasped at what they saw.

Cap't Rolly had a man tied to a chair with what looked like a clothesline.

He held a machete menacingly over the man's head.

“Who's he?” Ethel asked.

“Where are my children!” screamed Marge. “Where are they?”

Patti and the children came from the back of the house.

Jennifer and Bobby ran to their mother.

She wrapped their arms around her children like a hen guarding her chicks under her wings.

The RCMP officers entered the house and took in the scene.

Patti's hands and voice shook as she said, “He wanted us to eat that candy.” She pointed to a box of candy on the table.

“What's going on here?” an officer asked.

Patti took a deep breath. “He came to the door. He said he

was giving candy away as a promotion. But then he pushed his way into the house and tried to force the kids to eat it."

Bobby piped up. "It looked gross!"

"We remembered 'Stranger Danger,'" Jennifer said. "We're not supposed to take things from strangers. So we didn't. We crawled under the table to get away from him."

"Yeah, I took Q with us. She didn't like that guy either."

"Q hissed at him. When he got down to pull us out, Q attacked him and clawed his face."

"That's when I grabbed the kids and ran. We ran to the bathroom and locked the door. Thanks to Q, we got away."

Q sauntered out from her hiding place.

Ethel picked her up and cuddled her. "Good kitty," she murmured.

"That's about the time I got to the house," Cap't Rolly picked up the story. "I heard Patti yelling at the kids. I heard this guy yelling about the cat. He turned on me like he would fight me until he saw my machete. Then it was easy to get him to sit in the chair so I could tie him up."

The man sat silently, looking at his feet.

Ethel pointed at him. "Patti," she said. "We're so sorry for what happened here."

Patti grinned wearily. "You didn't know."

Marge said, "Can you take the kids to your house? They don't need to be here right now."

"Sure. I'd like to go home, anyway. Come on, kids. Hot cocoa and cookies at my house." She held out her hands to the children.

After they left, an officer asked, "Do you know this guy?"

They had untied him, handcuffed him, and left him sitting on the chair.

Marge shook her head.

Ethel cocked her head to one side and said, “Hmm. He looks familiar, but I cannot place where I may have seen him.”

The man raised his head and glared at Ethel. “You should know me. You're the one who killed my mother!”

Ethel frowned. “I've never killed anyone in my life! What are you talking about?”

“Yes, you did! The Adult Protective Services took her away from me and put her in your Lodge. It's because of you she died there!”

“When? I don't remember.”

“They said our home wasn't fit. They said I didn't care for her well enough. I cared! She was my mom!”

Suddenly, Ethel remembered the residents. “Was it your mom that the Health Department brought to the Lodge just over a year ago?”

“Yes.”

Ethel remembered thinking it was strange that the Health Department had brought the woman. Usually, they came on their own or their families brought them.

Ethel said, “I remember. I also remember what the orderlies told me. Your mom arrived in a filthy nightie. We had to bathe her four times to find the beautiful woman underneath all that filth. She was so weak, she couldn’t walk to the toilet or feed herself.”

She crossed her arms over her chest. “Your mom needed good food and constant care. Evergreen Lodge provided what she needed. She was in ill health when she arrived. Yet the end of her life was clean, well-fed, and happy. Although she asked often for you."

With a shock, Ethel realized that this woman's autopsy report was the one she pulled from the files. The one comparable to Steve's.

Looking away from him, she spoke calmly to the officers. "His name is George. He has mental issues. I remember him now. He clung to his mother like a baby when he visited her right before she died. In the six months she lived with us, that was the only time he visited. Look into her autopsy. I think he killed her, too."

George whimpered. "They took her when I was at the taco stand. I didn't know they took her. She belonged with me, not with you."

"What's this about the taco stand?" she asked.

"The taco stand is where I hang out. The owner likes me. He lets me fill in when he has to do something."

"Did you sell Steve tacos?" Ethel asked. "Did you sell me tacos?"

George nodded. "I made the special sauce. I put lots on the tacos."

"Where did you get the poison for your special sauce?" Cap't Rolly asked.

"From my cousin Will. He gave it to me. It's for fish and people."

"Why did you kill my husband?" Marge asked.

"She took my mom away from me," wailed George, pointing at Ethel. "It's all her fault! I wanted to take away someone she loved."

"By killing my son and me?"

An officer asked, "Did you put the poison in the candy?"

"Yes! And if you hadn't come, they all would be dead like my mom!" He looked at the box of candy on the table.

Marge stepped to the table to close the lid.

"Don't touch that," an officer said.

He donned gloves and put the box of candy in an evidence bag he pulled out of his pocket.

"We'll process this evidence and get his complete statement. We're through here."

Cap't Rolly said, "Two murders and four attempted murders is quite the charge against him."

"We'll lock him up for a long time. You can be sure of that."

"Let me ask him something. George, why did you poison the fish in Howe Sound?"

"To find out how much I needed to kill a person."

Cap't Rolly turned to the officers. "I'm a scientist. I've studied this poison. Handle the evidence with gloves. The poison has contaminated him, too. Part of his mental issues is from handling and breathing in the poison for a length of time. He's toxic. He might not live long enough to stand trial."

The officers put on disposable gloves before they escorted George to their car.

Ethel watched them walk away as Marge put on a pot of coffee and called Patti to tell her the 'coast was clear.'

The children ran into the kitchen and wrapped their arms around their mother again.

Marge winked at Ethel and Cap't Rolly. Turning to Patti, she said, "I have to go to town tomorrow. Do you think you could watch the kids?"

Patti turned on her heel and headed back to her house. Over her shoulder, she said, "Gee, I'm so sorry, but I have another engagement tomorrow."

The adults roared with laughter.

Grinning, Patti walked back into the kitchen.

"What's so funny?" Jennifer asked.

"Patti thinks hanging with us is dangerous." Marge wiped tears of laughter from her eyes.

The adults enjoyed a quiet cup of coffee while the children went into the living room to watch cartoons.

The trail to Secret Cove was quiet. No breeze. Nothing ruffled the leaves or the tranquility.

Patti left to go home.

Cap't Rolly stood to leave, also.

"I'll say good day to you, too." He looked at them. "Just to let you know, a friend of mine called and offered me a job at the University of Hawaii. I'll sail as soon as the weather changes."

The two women watched him walk out of their lives as he had come in the night Ethel invited him to dinner seven months ago.

Marge glanced at Ethel. "You never gave me an answer to the question I asked you last night."

"I'm thinking about it," Ethel replied as she took a sip of her coffee.

www.ingramcontent.com/pod-product-compliance
Lightning Source LLC
LaVergne TN
LVHW050555160826
845677LV00011B/2319

* 9 7 9 8 8 3 9 9 9 0 1 1 1 *